Like A Whisper In Your Ear
Aural Erotic Science Fiction

edited by Nobilis Reed

Circlet Press, Inc.
Cambridge, MA

For catalog, information about our imprints, review copies, and other information, please write to:

Circlet Press, Inc.
39 Hurlbut Street
Cambridge, MA 02138

Or visit us online at: http://www.circlet.com

Contents

Introduction
5

The Game by Cecilia Tan
7

When The Stars Come by Alex Picchetti
23

By The Book by Elizabeth Thorne
39

Outermost Claw, Front Right Foot by Steven Schwartz
53

Invasion! by Beverly Langland
69

Game Fae by Vivien Jackson
83

Runic Runaway by Michael M. Jones
97

Pow! Bash! Yes, Yes! by Sophie Mouette
117

Enchanted by Shanna Germain
125

Mistress Under the Hill by Annabeth Leong
133

Contributors
153

Introduction

There is an unusual sort of pleasure, to have a story read to you. It's a bit like the feeling of a massage, or the aromas of a meal being cooked for you. It's an experience crafted for your senses by one individual. But unlike a massage or a meal, a story conveys meanings and emotions that speak to us on a deep level. Music and dance can do the same thing, but not the way the spoken word does. For me at least, this experience is unique among all the arts.

It is for this reason that the anthology you are about to experience is unlike any other. The stories in this collection were not chosen to fit a particular theme, nor are they a 'best of' collection, though I am proud to be able to bring you every one of them. Instead, these stories were chosen for their appropriateness to being read aloud.

Not every story works well in audio. Some rely on the juxtaposition of words on a page, or rely on unusual symbols or typography. Others use language in a way that diverges from how people normally speak and listen, constructing complex structures of meaning that require close analysis and careful re-reading to bring full understanding. As fine as those stories can be, they have been left aside for this anthology.

As a result, this anthology contains perhaps the widest variety of stories ever published in a single Circlet Press anthology. We're bringing you everything from superhero rivalry-turned-ribaldry in Sophie Mouette's "Pow! Bash! Yes! Yes" to Lovecraftian erotic horror in Alex Picchetti's "When the Stars Come." In "Outermost Claw, Front Right Foot" we present the most self-consistent piece of high fantasy dragon erotica I've ever seen, and with "Enchanted" by Shanna Germain, a fairy tale retelling which beautifully maintains timeless mythological structure along with modern sensuality.

Due to a peculiarity of modern publishing, you may have picked up this book in text format and not in audio. If so, then consider this your invitation to give audio erotica a try; either read a story from this book to someone who will appreciate it, ask someone to read it to you, or else find the audio edition and listen to one of the talented voice artists I have selected. Because truly, this book is meant to whisper in your ear.

And moan, and grunt, and cry out.

Nobilis Reed
April 2018

The Game
Cecilia Tan

I met Marik during the last six months of my sentence, when I was assigned to a work pod at the space port to finish my indentured servitude. All a part of paying my "debt" to Malakaian society. There was Marik, Boolin, and me. Our official title was "mechanical service workers," mech techs, the people you see from your little round porthole running around on the tarmac tightening all the screws on the bucket you're trusting your life to, to take you up to light speed and beyond. We were all good at it, efficient, hard-working, maybe because we three enjoyed it. Marik and Boolin wore dark blue coveralls; I wore ash grey, because they were free and I wasn't. But among the three of us, it almost didn't matter. It never made a difference in our work. It only mattered in The Game.

Maybe it was my difference in status that sparked the Game in the first place. Being a convict on Malakai wasn't anything like being a legendary Kylaran sex slave, but ever since Malakai joined the Kylaran Federation, Kylaran ways had been infiltrating our culture. The Kylar kept pleasure slaves in an ancient and respected tradition, everyone knew that. They called them *caitan*.

Marik had initiated it that first time. We were required to be at the port whether there was any traffic or not, even when the stratostorms kept the skies closed for days. And Marik hated being bored. The three of us had nothing to do that afternoon but gab. We sat on a low bench in the workshop, talking about what life must be like for Kylaran overlords. "You could have a separate slave to wash each toe," Boolin was saying. "Every finger." I added, somewhat wistfully: "Yeah, or a different lay for every night of the week." Sex was forbidden for convicts, even after we'd been moved to the halfway dorms like I was. In prison, every night we were knocked out with sleep induction beds to keep us out of trouble.

Now that I was in my transition period, I was rubbing myself half raw every night, thinking about Boolin and Marik, Marik especially, who was quite my type. Boolin had midnight hair that he kept shoulder length like a lot of the city youths, made them look tough, like maybe they were ex-convicts. But he had a roundness to his face, and a open, friendly smile. Marik had the kind of harshness in his face that I found more than handsome. I stretched a little. "Just imagine, a different lay for every night of the year!"

Marik leaned his tough, small and wiry body against mine. "Or you could have just one who had to follow you every where, and give it up to you if you wanted it, whenever you wanted it."

I was grimy with machine lube and sweaty from the heat in the shop, my coveralls half open. I looked into his bird-of-prey eyes and couldn't quite breathe.

"They give you all your shots and immunizations when you get convicted, don't they?"

I nodded.

"But you don't get the benefits, do you. You're not allowed." He reached for my hand, and slid it toward the warmness of his crotch. I felt for his erection of my own accord and touching its spring steel hardness through the cloth—I wanted it. His voice dropped to a whisper. "How long has it been."

"Two years" I whispered in return. "I'm not allowed..."

He hushed me with a hand to my lips. "Let's just say I'm not giving you a choice. Are you going to put up a struggle?"

I didn't want to. I wanted him to fuck me silly. But I wasn't sure what he wanted me to do. "Should I?"

"Boolin," he said in a quiet voice. "Hold her arms."

Boolin came around to the other side of me and took hold of my wrists. He lay me down on the bench and held them above my head, while Marik opened the quick-seams of his coveralls and mine. His fingers dipped in to my crotch and he whistled. "You really are ready for it, aren't you."

I nodded and closed my eyes, hardly believing that we were

going to go through with this, but my only real fear was that he would stop.

He positioned himself over me and whispered into my ear. "Now remember, if anyone were to ever find out, we forced you to do this, right?"

"Right."

And he sank home.

That was as explicit as we ever got with words. From then on it was a delicate balance of things unspoken, even the attraction, the affection. We were buddies, we worked together, I could crank a turbine as fast as he could, he could spot a hairline in the ceramic as quick as me. We would have been equals, if I had been free. But I wasn't. And I never let myself think we were lovers, no matter how many times he plunged in to me. It went on that way, every few weeks there would be a break in the work and we'd indulge.

It got real serious one of those days when there was zero to do and traffic had been nil since the beginning of the week. From somewhere, Boolin had picked up a second-hand particle gun, and was cleaning it. Marik and I were hanging around, watching. Boolin began to brag, pointing the gun at the wall and sighting along his arm.

"Now this is what I call power," he said. "This thing'll rip the flesh off a human at over fifty lengths when it's powered up." It seemed so small, barely the size of his hand.

"Let me see it?" Marik held out a hand and Boolin tossed it across the workbench to him. "Nice." He made as if to pass it to me, then pulled back, remembering my status. "Uh uh, regulations say you're not supposed to come in contact with weapons," he said, a look of mock admonishment on his face.

"Yeah, and there's not supposed to be any weapons allowed in the port, either," I said, smiling sweetly.

"Oh, ho, ho, talking back. I think that's a punishable offense for a caitan under Kylaran law, isn't it?" He hefted the gun in his hand and pointed at the floor at his feet. "Kneel."

"No." I said it with enough fire in my eyes that he knew I meant no to his command, not no to The Game. It was a look that said Make Me Do It.

He grabbed me and I tried to spin away, but he held the gun to my throat, bending my head back. Out of the corner of my eye I could see Boolin, watching like he always did. Sometimes, under Marik's orders, I did favors for him, too. But his face had gone pale as he watched his gun plied against my throat.

"Down," Marik said, pushing the muzzle against the soft place under my chin. I went down inch by inch, as he held my hands behind my back with his other hand, bending backwards until I felt my knees touch the floor. He drew a line down my body then with the gun, straight down the center, ending at my crotch. He rubbed the muzzle in the space between my legs and I moaned.

"Marik, you bastard..." I couldn't say any more as the sensation swept over me and I closed my eyes. My whole pubic area began to ache and I felt the wetness starting to drip under my loose coveralls.

He grabbed me by my hair then and settled the gun against my forehead as he worked himself into a chair. He let go my hair to unclasp his coveralls from his neck down to his crotch and pulled his erection free. Keeping the gun against my skin, he fiddled with his free hand.

Boolin spoke in a whisper. "Don't! You're taking the safety off..."

"I know," Marik said, then to me, "You see this? I'm setting this open," he unlatched something, "so if my finger slips off this lever, or squeezes too hard, the weapon will fire. So it's your job to see that I don't go off half-cocked, right?"

I'm sure he was feeling the same rush I was, the fear was making me want him more than I'd ever wanted him before. This was more than breaking regulations. It was all I could do to keep from whimpering. I didn't answer.

"Suck me." He kept the gun on my forehead as I took him into my mouth. He leaned back in the chair, closing his eyes. I went at him with such zeal you would have thought sucking cock was my favorite thing. I had never liked it before I met Marik. But once we started playing The Game, I discovered I liked being forced to do it. And I was good at it, too. So Marik was happy to force me. I took him deep in, and let my tongue work his underside, all the time trembling under the hard pressure of the muzzle against my skull.

I felt him trembling, too, and gave second thoughts to the relish with which I was swallowing him. If he came too hard, he could slip... I almost stopped and told him to quit, but I kept on, more afraid of being called chicken, I guess, than of getting my head blown off.

When he came, his hand shook but his fingers stayed rigid. I spat out his semen onto the workshop floor. Even after all that, he couldn't get me to swallow. I sagged against the chair as he used his free hand to put the safety back on, and laid the gun down on the workbench. He hugged my head against his crotch, muttering an oath to himself. "That was..." he inhaled a huge gulp of air. "That was the best blow job of my life," he concluded.

I nodded, my clit throbbing so hard now I could hardly stay sitting on my knees like that. "Yeah..."

"Are you okay?" His eyes searched mine, and the corners of his mouth twitched. "Hot?"

"Yeah," I rubbed myself against his leg like a hungry pet.

He pulled me up into his lap and unclasped my coveralls as he had his own. Now I could see Boolin sitting on a bench against the wall. From the state of his clothes it looked like he'd jerked himself off already. Marik held me in his lap and let his arms circle around me, his hands burrowing down into my suit and between my legs. The first touch was like an electric shock. I gasped as he spread my lips with one hand and began tweaking my hard clit with the other. Then he slipped a finger inside me and began jiggling it furiously. He alternated between those two actions until I thought I would go mad. "Ah, come on, Marik, don't..."

"Don't what? Aren't you enjoying the torture? You forget you're not supposed to have a choice about this." He fingered my clit then, sawing his finger back and forth slowly.

I couldn't answer.

"I could stop, you know." He let his fingers rest.

"No! No, keep going..."

"Say please..."

"Please, oh please," Inspiration hit me then. "Please caishen," I used the Kylish word for master. "Please."

"Very well," he said and resumed the sawing motion, but faster this time. He'd learned by now that it was a good way to get an orgasm out of me.

He pushed me higher and higher. I clung to the arms of the chair, moving my hips as much as I could to help speed up the process. And then the Landing Signal blew. I cursed and started to move. Boolin jumped up and fastened his suit.

Marik held me fast. "Uh uh, I'm not letting you go 'til you're done." I tried to get up anyway, but his grip was too strong. We had to get out there or the monitors would get suspicious. He redoubled his efforts, "Come on, now, give yourself to me..." I leaned against him, letting him do the work. He whispered in my ear, "Come for me, come for me, my little caitan..." and I did, shaking the whole chair while his fingers didn't let up. And as the last tremor shook me he whispered, "You're mine."

It was a Kylaran interstellar transport coming in. Some kind of V.I.P. It had to be, for them to let it land during all the stratoference. Not that it made any difference to us. From the underside, all ships look about the same. But the chatter came over the link later, it was the overlord Bhujan, one of the high ranking Kylar, come to oversee the latest phase of transition to Kylaran law.

"What does that mean?" Boolin asked. "I mean, for you." He meant me, as an indentured.

"I haven't the slightest. You think they tell us anything?"

"Maybe," Marik said from where he sat on the work table, tossing a dirty rag toward me, "it means they'll let indentureds start having sex. To get them in shape for shipping off to the Kyl system and a life of sexual servitude."

I winged the rag back at him and it wrapped around his face. "Not bloody likely," I snorted.

That evening when I reported back to the dorm where I and fifty or so other female indentureds were kept until our terms ran out, I did find out a bit more, though. At the end of our meal period, an announcement came from the viewscreens that connected us to the warden's office. She, or rather what was probably just a graphic animation of her, came on and announced that tonight we would each find a sleep induction pad in place of our pillows. A routine psychiatric evaluation would take place while we slept.

"Wait a minute," I said when the screen had gone blank. "All of us at once?"

Harla, the big woman sitting next to me agreed. "Yeah. I know I'm not due for my next psych eval for another two months. I just had one last week!" She cursed and muttered. "It's violating our rights."

Jenna laughed from across the table. "Didja forget? While we're here, we don't have any rights."

"Maybe it has something to do with the new rules coming down," I said, more to myself than to any of the others. That had to be the explanation.

"What new rules?"

"There's a new Kylaran overlord coming in." None of the others knew anything about it but me. "They're supposed to institute new laws. Kylaran laws." We weren't allowed to speculate much more after that as they ushered us off to our rooms and locked us in for the night.

The next morning, there was a warden waiting for me. My first thought was, oh shit, I'm busted. Someone found out about me and Marik. But I tried to play it cool. "What's this about?"

"Job interview," was all she said, and indicated a clean set of clothes at my feet. "Wash up as usual, get dressed, and present yourself downstairs."

Job interview? Well, the whole point of the indenture program was supposed to be to get convicts like me back into society, reformed and no longer a burden. Maybe they had found me something better. But it didn't sound like it would be something better. The space port job was pretty good as it was, plus what I had with Marik was better than anything I'd ever had before.

Downstairs there was a transport waiting to take me and six others somewhere. None of us spoke, just looked at each other with glances that said 'I don't know either.' We were driven to one of the palatial houses in the diplomatic sector. I swore under my breath. Maybe Marik was, perversely, correct when he said we were going to be shipped off. The others looked at me, but I said nothing.

They separated us into different rooms in the house and then I was alone with my speculations. I was in a bedroom, an unoccupied one from the look of it. The table by the bed was bare and so was the clothes chest. There were two chairs by the window and I sat in one. Judging by the sun, hours went by while I sat there, wondering what Marik and Boolin were doing, and whether the wardens sent someone else in my place.

I had dozed off near midday when the sound of the door opening made me jerk awake. A man with soft blond hair and broad shoulders came in. Since he was alone, I thought at first that he must be someone sent to fetch me. But then I saw the way he carried himself, and the way he was looking at me. I would have thought an overlord would be followed by servants everywhere.

He sat down in the other chair and his breath sounded a little weary. "So you are Syn."

"Yes."

"Say 'yes, my lord' and you'll please me."

"Yes, my lord," I said, without feeling.

"Your file says you were a non-violent offender, and that in two months you'll be free."

It didn't seem like that required an answer so I didn't give one.

"Are you looking forward to being free, Syn? To being your own woman again?"

"It beats prison," I joked. "My lord."

He smiled a droll smile. "Is there something else you'd prefer?"

I knew where this had to be leading. There could be no other explanation for the way his eyes roved over me in my soft gray tunic and leggings. But I played dumb. "I'm not sure what you mean, my lord."

He stood, walked until he was behind me, and began to stroke my hair. "I think you do." I sat without moving while he ran his hands through the cropped short mass of hair and over the back of my neck. "I'll be very direct with you now, Syn. I am Bhujan, an overlord of the first order of the Kylar, and I want you for a caitan."

I hate it when I'm right, sometimes.

"I need a Malakaian caitan. It sets an example for your people. And I think you could be, oh, such a prime example."

"Why me, my lord?" He couldn't know about me and Marik. He couldn't. He only arrived yesterday.

"Because of your deep potential. You have depths of submission that only a true master can bring out."

The psych scan. Last night was no ordinary psych scan. "I don't know what you mean," I said again, my lip trembling a little bit.

"I shall have to show you, then." He pulled my head back with firm fingers against my chin, so that now I looked him in the eye. Something told me he could be very convincing. "I know your true nature."

I trembled a little as he pulled me to my feet and carried me to the bed. The psych scan was a Kylaran technology in the first place, and common rumor was that it had been developed in the for evaluating the suitability of slave stock. They could tell who would turn disloyal and in how many years, who was lazy, who would harbor secret resentment. If Bhujan really knew that I had it in me to be a caitan, who was I to question?

The Game, I thought, as he began discarding my prison-grey clothing. The Game was only a taste of it. Maybe I was destined for this, to live the real thing.

"A caitan is not permitted to cover her body in the presence of her caishen," he said as he stripped away the last of what I wore. "She, or he, is expected to be, at all times, ready for service."

That sounded like a cue to me. But what was I supposed to do now? Tell him how ready I was? I didn't feel particularly ready. I felt mostly scared, my mind awhirl with possibilities and wondering how this would be different from The Game. If it were Marik, he would have already manipulated me into a state of such desire that I would be begging him to use me already. Bhujan said he was going to show me the depths of my submission, was he not? Prove it to me, I thought. Prove to me that there's something even deeper and better than the Game. "And what if the caitan isn't?" I asked, in what I hoped was a timid and inquisitive voice.

"Then he or she pays the price of not being ready," he said as he turned me over onto my stomach and forced my legs apart. I felt his cock pressing against the far too dry cleft of my labia and then, holding me still by my shoulders and neck, he thrust up into me.

I made an injured sound into the pillow where my head pressed. His weight was full upon me now, and his arms snaked around and held me to him as he pushed in and out. "You have the flesh of the Kylar inside you now. A great honor."

I gritted my teeth and spat out "It hurts."

"Honor usually does," he said as he pulled out, and I sighed with relief.

One of his hands was on my back now, pressing me down, and I could feel the soft loose cloth of his sleeve. The other caressed my buttocks. "You see," he explained, his voice still as calm as ever, "you will serve me today whether you choose to or not. You are the state's property and I am the state, now."

And then he gave me a hard smack across the buttocks. I

gasped but did not cry out. "You are mine to do with as I will. Whether I hurt you," another hard blow landed, "or whether I force you to pleasure because it pleases me." He began to hit me harder, although I hadn't thought that possible, blow after blow sending shock up my spine and making me want to scream out the pain, although I didn't.

I don't know how long that went on. I lost track of the blows and the sensation of my whole body becoming disconnected from the pain began to grow. And then I felt his fingers sliding down the hotness of my ass, between my legs again.

He was pleased and I was surprised to find I was dripping wet now. Maybe Bhujan did know more about how I worked than I did. No one had ever hit me like that before and I'd no idea that it would get me wet. I was puzzling out how that might work, what was it in spanking that caused me to lubricate like that? Especially since I wasn't hungering for his cock the whole time? Marik would have been running the cock up and down my leg this during the affair, making sure I knew just what was coming next and how he was making me wait for it.

Bhujan turned me onto my back again. I could see how his robes opened to free his groin without making him seem naked or vulnerable. "Do you understand," he said "that I did not have to stop before. I could have just gone on until I was satisfied. But sometimes the master must be sure that his slave enjoys the honor of his cock inside her. If she does not, she must be trained to enjoy it. She must be punished if she does not. Do you understand, now?"

I didn't. Did he mean he spanked me to punish me for not being wet enough for him? How did he know that would have the right effect though? He was waiting for some kind of answer. I avoided his question. "I am ready for you now, my lord." As ready as I'd ever be, I suppose.

This time he slid in slowly, letting my cunt suck him in bit by bit as if it knew what it wanted. As my hips moved of their own accord to let him sink deep to the hilt, I wondered again, perhaps he did know me better than I seemed to know myself.

It felt good to have him inside me, that much I had to admit. The soreness of before was barely noticeable as he dragged himself in and out with slow, deliberate strokes.

"Do you know why the tradition of keeping caitan was begun?" he asked me as he stroked in, then out, his eyes closed.

"No, my lord."

"I will tell you then. When the Kylar were first beginning their conquests of the other lands on our home world, ages and ages ago, the overlords were a special breed of men and women. We were raised and bred to have a certain temperament, attitude and aptitude, that suited us to conquering our neighbors."

One might say, *rapacious*, I thought.

"Part and parcel with the inborn zeal for conquest came other desires and needs so overwhelming that they could, in some, be a detriment. Over the generations, it came to be known that the overlords' physical needs for combat and for sexual satiation were inseparable. Likewise, their psychological needs to own, annex and dominate."

It made a great deal of sense. But I wondered how he could go on that way, his voice still and calm, even cold, as it had been when we were sitting by the window. His rhythm never broke, in his speaking nor in the way he was rocking in and out of me.

"In the caitan, there is a very special task then, to serve the overlord is to support the greater glory of the Kylar. To quench the fires that burn in him, to contain his energy, to be the receptacle of his emotions, whether that means to suffer through pain, use, or even pleasure."

With the long strokes the way he was making them there was no way I could come, although I was pushed constantly closer and closer to the edge. Each time he sank in there would be a brief moment of pressure on my clit, and then just the stoking of the fire deep inside.

"The best caitan come to realize their place and their importance and they give up everything, even their own will, to serve the greater end. They know without fail that it is their mission to serve, because there is no other time, no other place when they feel that power flowing through them, no other time when they have touched God."

For all his pompous words, I could not picture Bhujan as the embodiment of a god, not even Zal or Kyl, the gods of dominance and submission. His words put me back to thinking about Marik. Marik who didn't seem to need all these words to make his point.

Bhujan took a small device out of his robe and placed it against my forehead. "All your choices have been taken away. Now I choose when you come and how many times." He pressed it and the orgasm that had been building so very slowly over all this time exploded through me, making my legs shake, my eyes roll back and my throat hoarse as I cried out wordlessly.

When I went limp he was still stroking in and out as if nothing had happened. I had never come like that in all my life.

"You have pleasure only because it pleases your master that you do." He hit the button again and again I was rocketed through a bone-shaking orgasm. His hand sought out my clit, which by now was so hypersensitive I couldn't bear him to touch it, but of course I had to bear it, I could not move or pull away from him, impaled on him like that.

"No, don't..." I said, before I could stop myself.

"Ah, my little caitan," he said, and my spine went cold at how that phrase reminded me of Marik, "now you begin to learn." And he hit the button again.

It was like electric shock coming through my clit and I screamed. And yet, it was pleasure, so much pleasure that it burned like I never knew nerves could burn. Incredible, it was, but I wasn't sure if I could take any more of it. "You see how it is," he breathed, "when you have no choices. You know I can force you to do anything, anything at all, even betray your own body with pleasure."

"Yes, yes!" I said, not because I agreed but because I hoped I'd get a little rest if he went off on another little lecture. I thought of Marik, the way Marik had forced me to come just yesterday when the landing signal went off. And the way, once I had come, he had

whispered 'you're mine' just as if it was an irrefutable truth.
Bhujan buried himself in me now, no longer moving, and I could
feel him holding himself back from orgasm. Marik, I thought,
Marik, did you mean it when you said that? Marik did not need
any Kylaran technogadget to bend my body to his will. And it came
to me that surrender was not something truly forced. It was,
ultimately, a choice that had to be made.

Bhujan was speaking to me still. "Now you have had a taste of
it. You know I can force you to do anything. Now I will ask you to
make one final choice in your lifetime."

"What is that, my lord?"

"Will you be my caitan? Do you understand the choice you
make?"

I did. If I surrendered to him, then he had truly cowed me,
whereas if I continued to resist, although he could force me to do
anything he wanted, he could not truly own me. It was true, he
had shown me how deep my submission could go.

And despite all his manipulations, I was not cowed. The only
question that remained in my mind was, what would he do to me
if I said no? Kill me? Put me back into prison? I could feel his
exalted Kylaran flesh throbbing inside mine, but I knew I could
not betray Marik. Marik, to whom I truly belonged, I could not
betray him by giving myself to this pompous ass. I was not my
own to give.

"I understand the choice I make." I said. "I will not be yours."

Bhujan's calmness cracked like an egg leaking poison. He
gripped me by the shoulders and with an animal cry of fury he
began to come. He pistoned in anger and frustration until he
pinioned me with his arms, his weight and his coming, his
precious Kylaran seed filling me and overflowing from me as he
jerked away.

As I lay there, feeling as if I might never move again, he said
"I am almost tempted to keep you anyway, to see if I couldn't break
you." He fastened up his robes and picked the little orgasm inducer
off my forehead. "But I haven't the time." He left shaking his head,
as if he still could not figure out where he had gone wrong.

He was a spiteful bastard after all that. When I returned to the dorm they informed me I was being transferred to a higher security facility up the coast in another district, for three months of "observation." After that was over, I would have my six months of indentures, no chance I would be at the space port again now that I was in another geographic jurisdiction, and then, I would be free.

I prayed at night that Marik and Boolin were just as I'd left them, tinkering in the overheated little shop and jerking each other off when things got dull, and that when I was given back my citizenship I could find them there, and join them, and things would be as they had been. It was less than a year, what could change in a year? I prayed, and prayed, to Kyl, the god of slaves, that I was not wrong about this, that I would never be free again.

When the Stars Come
Alex Picchetti

I know what the townsfolk thought of me. They called me fanciful and more than a little dull-witted, but that was their own foolishness; I had no need to speak to them, and so played at being the mad-eyed yokel's daughter. Maybe I was, once, that silly girl; but now my mind is clear.

They thought my father took me, that Hallowe'en night in the circle, or the least imaginative of them did. The truth is my father would not have dared to soil the Beyond One's vessel. He was at most an onlooker, although he tells me naught could be seen beyond the brightness of the holy stars.

You are afraid. I can feel it on you. Let me tell you my story.

My mother was a religious woman, in the traditional sense. I sometimes wondered how she came to be married to my father, who liked to tell me the few stories he knew from the Necronomicon, especially those of Yog-Sothoth. My mother hated those stories, told my father they were too dark for anyone, let alone a little girl. Why they terrified her more than the pastor's tales of the seals breaking and trumpets sounding, I couldn't understand. My father simply shrugged, but after several days of my dreaming of the beings described by the prophet Alhazred, my mother put her foot down and demanded that no more tales be told.

I craved the stories. The dreams, if anything, became more vivid; but when I tried to tell my father of them, he shushed me and reminded me my mother had forbidden us to talk of The Lurker at the Threshold. It became clear to me that action was necessary.

Anyone who has worked on a farm will tell you that pigs are incredibly stupid creatures, though still able to outwit your average farmhand. And even in those days, we rarely had visitors; my father made most folk uneasy, whereas my mother was simply unkind.

And so, when my father was away on business one week in the fall, I hatched my plan.

It came to me in a dream.

I found myself submerged totally in the icy grip of the lake. Ice crackled thick above me. I was trapped. The cold crushed my chest. Breathing was impossible. Beyond the frost I could see the dancing of beautiful lights in the trees, beckoning me. My hands were like lead, but I pounded as hard as I could to break free. There was no use.

Just as I thought I must die, something brushed against my hand. A knife, long and curved and wicked. I stabbed it into the ice and the ice bled, the heat of it warming my hands and giving me strength. I carved through it, felt it give way as though it were lard to a hot blade.

I pulled myself onto the surface of the ice, the freezing water running down my thighs and snapping as I came into the frozen air. Above the lake, the stars glowed a color that I cannot describe. They swam and danced in the sky, moving to unheard music before plummeting, one, two, then twenty, then a thousand; they filled the sky and crashed to the earth around me, shattering the thick coat of frost that sealed the earth in slumber. I laughed until one flew into my mouth.

I awoke shivering, sweat making the sheets cold and clingy. The world outside my window was gray and dull, with no sign of the beautifully alien stars.

I knew, with clarity, what I was meant to do.

I could hear my mother outside, feeding the livestock. I dressed quickly to stave off the chill; uncertain what to do with the damp sheets, I folded the quilt back over and hid the offending spot.

In the barn, the cows chewed their cud as I searched for my tool. I didn't think I could overpower my mother, so I would need to rely on speed and surprise. Finally, my hand curled around the handle of the butchering knife.

I left her in the sty. The pigs were glad of a hot meal.

When my father returned, three days later, I sat him down in his favorite chair by the fire and brought him dinner and tea. I took his boots and set them by the fire to warm and, when he had finished his meal, I took his plate and brought him the book.

He ran his fingers over it, slowly, as though savoring the texture of the cover, which was always slightly warm to the touch. His eyes met mine steadily.

"That was quite a meal. You do that yourself?"

"Yes."

"Where's your mother at?"

I didn't answer, but I didn't break his gaze either.

After a minute, he nodded. "Lavinia..."

"She was holding us back, Pa," I said, the words tumbling furiously out. "We know it, both of us! With her dead god-man and her worries about this world and the next. Who cares about this world? Yog-Sothoth is beyond it in all directions and times. He's bigger than her god for sure."

"Well." He sighed. "You're right about that, at least." He rubbed at the bridge of his nose. "Where is she, Lavinny?"

"What's left is still in the sty," I said, quietly.

He nodded, sighed again. "We'll have to go into mourning," he said finally. "You got to be careful with the townspeople, Lavinny. Gossip's one thing, but people lookin' too close is another. You understand?"

I nodded.

He spent the night building the coffin, and finding the remaining pieces of my mother to put in it. I watched him from my upstairs window, too excited by the possibilities to sleep; but I gained some understanding of my father, for he built that coffin carefully, and placed her bits in so gently, that I felt almost sorry for what I had done.

Finally, in the small hours before dawn, I slept. In my dreams, a creature of shadow came to me, speaking the language of the stars. I could feel the one inside me pulsing in response, almost as if I could speak back to it. It was thankful to me. One hand, if I could call it that, trailed down my cheek, soft as blowing smoke.

After my mother's death, life became much busier for me. One thing I hadn't considered in my youthful fervor was exactly how instrumental my mother was to the farm. My father was pleasantly useless, used to handling only the business aspects of things and being content to let my mother work her magic otherwise, and I was barely a woman. I did what I could, and my father never seemed to mind much that the farm suffered in her absence, although he would visit the cemetery more frequently than I liked.

Instead of farming, he dedicated himself to translating more of the Book. Rather than church on Sundays, we would spend our time reading the stories we knew and working on the ones we didn't. I developed something of a talent for Latin, as my father's edition had only fragments of the English text. Every so often he would visit the university to copy bits we were missing and, as time went on, we began to reveal the secrets for many rites to The Beyond One. What little free time I had I spent wandering the hills, mumbling fragments to myself, turning over the meanings in my head to try and achieve the most perfect realization of Alhazred's words, and fantasizing about the smoke creature and the alien stars, who had never left my dreams. Indeed, sometimes I swore could feel the star I had swallowed that night in my body, traveling within it, seeking a place.

The farm foundered. The pigs and cattle my father would buy never seemed to be as healthy as one could hope. Perhaps it was my fault, as I was driven to distraction by my quest for knowledge, but the piglets didn't thrive and the calves were skin and bones. But my dreams grew more vivid as I grew older, pushing me forward in my quest. The dream creature wanted me to learn something, and I was utterly devoted to its desires.

I ignored the townspeople, their snickering laughs and the pointing fingers of their children. On the rare occasion that I was called upon to make small talk, I'm sure I must have sounded quite simple, as I never bothered to keep abreast of the goings-on of these people that I cared very little for. Thankfully my strange looks and stranger mannerisms kept most people away, especially the young men; and as my former schoolmates became young women and married and had children, I remained happily devoted to my texts and my strange gods.

It was shortly after my twenty-first birthday that I made the breakthrough.

My father, knowing me well, had brought me a new fragment from the university text as my gift. The language was thick and difficult, and I suspect that my father may have copied some parts incorrectly, or they had been blurred out; I had worked several Sundays on it and had even taken to dreaming about the page of words.

In one of those dreams, I saw a subterranean cavern, elegantly carved as though it were the inside of a snail shell. At the center of the shell, a hundred figures danced in flickering torchlight and, as they danced, the ceiling began to shudder and churn.

I crept closer, keeping to the shadows, although I didn't think they could see me. I began to see in more detail: the deep, rich colors of their flowing garments, in styles I did not recognize. Then more detail still: the odd shape of their heads, the glint of scales in the light. Their elbows and knees bent in ways that were not right for men, allowing them graceful and daring movements as their frenzy built.

Then the singing began.

It began as a susurrus, so low and sweet I thought a wind was sweeping through; the ceiling crackled above, and crumbled dust fell upon us, dousing the lanterns and coating the reptile-men in a strange glow. Now I could see the starlight above, though I was certain that we were far too deep in the earth for such a thing to be possible.

The chanting rose, the creatures calling back and forth, something between screaming and music, *ia! ia!* One of them broke free of the circle, spinning her way to the center of the group, leaping on top of a raised dais. There she spun and gyrated, alone, calling down the gods with voice and body.

And as she sang, the star within me began to throb between my thighs.

I collapsed at the intense sensation, my hands flying to my skirt to pull it up. Above me, the stars shifted wildly, changing into unrecognizable constellations, pulsing and vibrating. The crescendo of ecstasy from the dancers peaked as I pushed my bloomers aside to press my hand between my legs.

The stars began to fall, and a gentle breeze began to pick up, swirling dust and stars together around the dais as the woman continued to dance. Sometimes a star would whisper across her body and she would keen. My fingers pushed against the hard nub between my legs and I gasped, arching.

Suddenly the dancers fell to their knees, silent and prostrate as the dust and stars took on a shape, human-like and yet not at all human; strands of pearlescent hair floating above a hazy figure, monstrously large fingers tipped with stars. The creature from my dream, so many years ago.

Its fingers slid down the unnaturally long curve of the reptile-woman's neck, pushing aside her garment as its hair-tendrils intertwined with the long spines around her face, pulling her towards it. On the floor of the cave, I shoved away my own clothes, stifling hot, as those immensely long fingers stroked along her spine. It dipped closer to her and, with the voices of the hundred reptile dancer men, it whispered its powerful sweet words.

Her tail thrashed wildly, and her tongue slithered out to taste the blue electric power of those pulsating stars. She let it slide between the fork of her tongue, circled it tantalizingly slowly; the creature drew her ever closer, until she took the orb into her mouth and swallowed it whole.

As she writhed in its grip, consuming its very being, I sought my own destruction on that subterranean floor. My fingers pressed against that throbbing nub of flesh, then into the space beyond, as tears streamed down my face. Each time she took a constellation into her, the cavern shook with a force that rocked me harder against my hand. I moaned then, and though the still dancers never took their eyes from the queen and their god, I felt the presence's attention shift to me, its last, giant orb watching as I shuddered through the most terrifying, ecstatic moment of my life, even as she swallowed it whole. I came utterly undone.

I awoke to the pounding of blood in my head and through my nether regions. Hesitantly I reached to touch myself as I had in the dream and rapidly had to muffle the sound of my gasping with my pillow. I probed and dipped my fingers into the wetness there and rapidly brought myself to another dizzyingly intense climax. I burned in my nightclothes despite the coldness of the winter; each brush of the sheets and garments against my body sent me into further spasms. I thought that perhaps now, having seen the face of my strange god, I was to die like this.

It was only after my father came to check on me that I was able to stop compulsively touching my body. I snatched up the text fragment and brandished it at him as he stood at my bedside, a worried frown on his face.

"It's the ritual, Pa," I told him. "The one for calling Him down. That's why I can't figure it out!"

"Lavinny, you're all red," he said, placing a hand on my cheek. "You're burning up, m'girl."

"I'm fine," I insisted. "Pa, you hafta get more o'this. It's right here, I know it. But this is just the chant. They were spinning, so beautifully..."

He tucked me firmly into that bed and told me he would bring some tea up. My father may have been a passable wizard in his own right, but he was a little scared of me.

If possible, I became even more enamored of my work. My father, bless him, listened to my ravings and set about visiting Miskatonic University when he could; but the folks there didn't like him much, and so it took him nearly six months to get the part we needed.

I'm sorry to say that the farm pretty well failed that year, for I spent all my time either in bed or on the Hill exploring this new relationship with the piece of Yog-Sothoth in my body. I could feel its presence in me, sometimes in my nipples as they grew hard to my touch, and sometimes in the tip of my tongue when I licked my own skin; and, of course, always when I let my fingers trail down my belly and between my thighs, the star inside me would follow. I began to take more notice of the local boys and girls, and their interactions—and it was in this way that I discovered that the boys called this the girl's cunt—and I secretly began to observe their doings. I was a shadow, below their notice, and I watched them rut like dogs in stables or hidden in the forests sometimes. I saw the girls get pregnant and married, and I asked their mothers pointed questions. They laughed nervously through their answers and were vague; they thought me an idiot, a pitiable creature without a mother to tell her the ways of the world.

I did not care. I was preparing for The Beyond One's coming.

When my father finally puzzled out the facts of the ritual, it was disappointing news. "Not for another thirteen years, Lavinny," he said sadly. "We hafta wait for the Moon to line up just right with Neptune, and she's a wobbly one, I'm afraid."

"When?" I asked.

"All Hallow's, so it'll be a cold night, too."

"I don't care," I told him firmly.

"You know, Lavinny..." He seemed abashed. "I know it's been strange, with your ma gone all these years. But you're a grown girl now. Don't you think you might want to... you know, settle down, like?"

"Get married, have children?" I gave him a look of utter contempt. "Pa, no boy in the area wants a thing to do with me, and no mother anywhere would let her son so much as look my way. And anyway, I have no interest in wasting my time on them! I have done everything in my life to get this." He looked unconvinced. "Wouldn't you rather be father-in-law to the Gate and the Key, not Chauncey Sawyer from down the way?" I knelt next to him, begging now. "Pa, listen. The nuns all take their vows for their Lord and no one says a word agin' 'em. Why can't I do the same for my god?"

He patted my hair gently. "If you're sure."

"I've never been this sure of anything ever."

He smiled proudly, his eyes bright, and gave me a kiss on the forehead.

Thirteen years is a long time to wait for something.

Sometimes I would dream of the dancers under the stars, but it never had the intensity of the first vision. I spent my days reading what stories we had or watching my father figure out how to perform the ritual as a solitary warlock—was it better to draw out the pattern in fire or rocks beforehand, or move through the motions alone? What was the exact moment the stars would fall into alignment? What part of the ritual did I have to perform? How were we to purify the site for The Beyond One's arrival? What was I to wear?

The more time passed, the more it seemed to stretch out like poured molasses. We began inventing questions just to spend our time finding the answers.

I continued my self-education. The star within me guided my hands, and I became more and more aware of it as time passed. Some days it would bring intense sensitivity to my nipples, so that merely wearing a dress was like being stroked by a lover. Oftentimes it would stay in my cunt, waiting for me to provoke it with my fingers, or stroke soft linens against it. But sometimes it would travel to the most unusual places, such as my heel (which made walking on the summer grass barefoot delightful) or my shoulder (which made being patted by a matronly old woman in town fraught and a little disturbing). Sometimes the type of touch mattered more, as pinching, biting, or slapping myself created exquisite pleasure. I never knew from day to day what the right combination would be and spent hours trying to find out. By the end of the thirteen years, I knew more about my body than I expect any woman alive did.

As for spying on the lovestruck locals, I discovered that, by and large, the girls didn't have quite the same intense response to their sexuality that I had. The boys who could bring them to that sort of shrieking, shuddering pinnacle of ecstasy were quite popular and usually married young. One boy in particular I stole ideas shamelessly from, probing my ass with a finger that night as I fondled my own breasts, imagining fingers long enough to wrap around my body, long enough that no amount of pushing would get all of it into that sweet spot. Later, one of the girls he had pleasured that way knelt in front of him, putting her mouth over his hard cock, and it was all I could do not to start masturbating in the loft I was hiding in, imagining my lover in his place; when his seed spattered on her lips and the barn floor, I saw only stars.

When that girl became pregnant, I realized that I would have to investigate the ins and outs of childbearing. My mother had always been the one to handle the farm; my father had helped in calving perhaps once, and at any rate the cows we had were so frail that giving birth was simply impossible. And I felt that my own pregnancy was likely to be somewhat different, at any rate. So I spent a lot of time around that family, asking my simple questions and getting my answers. I wonder what they might have thought if they had known how that knowledge would be put to use!

I wandered Sentinel Hill frequently, driving men away with my intense stare and half-mad babbling. All faked, of course, but this place was to become my church, chapel, and marriage bed someday; I wanted it unsullied by my mother's people and their superstitious, simple ways. In the summers I lay out in the sun all day until I became red and burned; in the winters, I bundled up to watch the stars and seek any sign of my love's universe. None came.

It took until the summer of 1912 before the reality of what my father and I were bringing about became all-consuming. I sat down with my meager sewing skills to fashion my dress; Arkham cloth was not up to the task of recreating the lizard-woman's dress, but I did what I could with what I had. The colors may not have been as vibrant or the workmanship as good, but I put that dress on at least once a day to stare at my own reflection. My father drew up his charts again, double-checking his work daily. He was so afraid that, after all of this time, his spells would not work, and nothing I said could soothe his anxiousness.

We spent the better part of August building the circle of runes that would serve for the ritual and the stone table to sit at the center of it, the two of us hauling heavy stone up the hill at midnight so as not to be bothered by prying eyes. My father did not want me to work, for it left my hands chafed and bleeding; but I insisted that Yog-Sothoth would be pleased at my dedication to him. Still, I spent September wrapped in bandages, and avoided the town except to buy liniment for the wounds.

I practiced my dance, now, hating that my body didn't have the sinewy grace of the lizard-woman, that my arms and legs did not bend in her ways. My own nervous energy made my usual means of distracting myself impossible, and the star itself seemed to have gone into hibernation, for I could not find it no matter how hard I tried. What orgasms I managed to have, after hours of working, were weak affairs, barely more than a tremble compared to the earth-shaking release of the others. Frustration is too gentle a word for how I felt; I was in agony, consumed with rage at the world, that it continued to keep me from my destiny for so long.

All Hallow's Eve was bitterly cold that year, and I spent the day sweeping snow off the ritual space, shivering against the icy winds. When I returned to dress, my father presented me with the last purchases of our tiny family fortune: a necklace of twisted metal protruding out like a sunburst, each ray tipped with rounded yellow-green gems, and a ring with the same gems set in. I kissed him.

"I din' want you to look too plain," he said. "This is a big day. 'S not every man gets to give his little girl away to a god."

"No," I said, and kissed him again. "You're too good to me, Pa."

"Whatever it takes for my little girl," he said humbly.

We waited until eleven o'clock before we wrapped ourselves in our coats and blankets, heated by the fire. My legs were like ice when I stepped out the door, the fine fabric of the dress doing nothing against the harsh conditions. I huddled further under the heavy coat and pulled the blanket closer around me. The walk was silent; my father reading his notes for the millionth time, and me stuck in a state of awestruck anticipation.

The stars glowed brightly in the black sky, mirrored in the

snow on the ground. My father pointed out the red dot of Mars in the sky, and checked his watch again. With two minutes until midnight, he helped me out of my jacket, and rubbed my bare white arms to warm me.

"You're a good girl, Lavinny," he said. "I'm so proud of you." He kissed me on the forehead. "Go on, now. It's almost time."

We took our places.

My father's voice echoed out over the hill. I always thought of him as a meek man, overrun by my mother, and then by me; but his voice was sonorous and commanding as he recited the tale of Yog-Sothoth, who was apart from the universe, who existed before it came into being, and would outlive it. His voice rasped in the tongue of the Elder Gods, who were the first to live in this world and gave the lizard-men the power of speech. He demanded the stars and the sky bear witness to this day, when Yog-Sothoth would come again to the world and bear his mark upon it. He stamped his feet and beat his walking-stick upon the ground, counting time.

I began to dance.

From that moment, it was as if there were nothing in the world but me and the ground and the stars above, pulsing in time with my heartbeat, all things echoing together with the pounding of blood in my ears. As if from a distance, I could hear my father calling up to the heavens to draw their attention to me, to watch my body spin through the air in a wild, frantic spasm of pure joy. The ice-cold winds I had felt were nothing to me now; I burned from inside with a wild flame, springing directly from my feet.

My star began to throb.

A curtain of blown snowflakes whirled around me, soft as any sheet, winding between my fingers and about my legs, gripping my hips like a desperate lover. I cried out my own ritual wish for the god:

Ia, ia, Yog-Sothoth, come down to me,
From wherever you come I seek you.
Lurker at the Threshold,
I charge you, open your gates to me,

Unlock me with your key.

The frost spun up to a wild tempest, scouring my skin clean, tearing at my dress, and the stars shattered above me in brilliant display until the constellations were unrecognizable, pieces of that awful sky falling to the dead earth and rising again.

My beloved had come.

I trembled and shivered as its tendrils wove firmly into my hair and around my thighs. My breath puffed up little clouds between us, giving the stars that were its eyes a halo of unnatural light.

You are the one that lets me in? it asked, probing my skin beneath the neckline of my bodice. A little jolt went through me, and I gasped and nodded. *You have waited a long time for me.* It began to peel the dress away, the seams tearing despite its gentle, slow movement. I whimpered a little as it tugged my hair gently, pulling my head back to expose my neck as it removed more layers of my clothing. *Yet I have been with you all this time.* One of its appendages curled around my leg and probed, gently, at the star in my cunt.

I keened and buckled, but its strong body held me up as I thrashed my way to climax, the proximity of our bodies enough to keep me orgasmic for what felt like an age. I came to pieces, lost everything except the knowledge of its presence. My arms felt boneless and limp. It finished undressing me, each of its feelers stroking so softly along my skin.

When I came again to my senses, or what little of them I could regain, I reached forward to take its face in my hands. It seemed bemused by this, but allowed me to explore it with my fingers, memorizing its features. Despite its smoky appearance, it had an odd sort of solidity to it, like water, and a cold, pulsating beat when my fingers dipped into the wreaths of its haze. It pulled harder on me when I did that, forcing me to bend back painfully; yet it also began to sprout more feelers, winding them between my toes and wrapping them, the strong trunks around my legs pulling them further apart. Several of the stars detached and rolled over my skin, little balls of hot ice rolling over me, freezing my nipples and then superheating them, sliding up my spine and leaving me begging for release. I was ready to die like that, wrapped in its arms, serving its alien desires.

Do you open your gates to me?

"Always," I gasped.

It caressed my lips, then probed gently into my mouth. I could feel the same happening to my cunt, its haze enveloping the rest of my body, a wispy sensation curling up my back and over my buttocks, my thighs squeezed tightly in its grip. It was as though three creatures had me pinned between them, each more fantastic than the last. One of the orbs rolling over me burrowed its way into my rear opening, and I bucked against it. It began to rhythmically pump into me, filling me with its being; and, just when I thought I was at the brink of orgasm again, it pushed me higher and higher into that feeling until all I knew was the precipice, the feeling of being about to fall or fly or crash and die.

One for you and one for me. Someday you will be the key. You will know as you have known all things. We are as one.

I awoke on Candlemas 1913 to labor pains that shook me horribly; my father ran to my bedside and cast some sort of spell, so that the dogs and whippoorwills screamed my pain for me. I could feel the two stars moving within me, crying to break free until finally they slid forth, my father acting as doctor and priest and midwife, cradling first Wilbur, as we later decided he should be called, and then his twin; my father and I agreed that no human name could possibly be suitable, and to leave that custom to the other side of his parentage.

It is impossible to say that I did not love my children. Who could not love the children of the god I so loved? I showed Wilbur the place of his conception, when he was old enough, and showed them both the various rites that we held. But I longed to once again be with The All-in-One, and become part of its All once more. And so, the year the twins turned thirteen—and what strapping young things they were, so like their father—I returned to the site of their conception, fourteen years to the day, and spoke to the sky, "I shall be a key for your gate, my love."

And I have never been heard from on Earth again, until now. So hear me when I say that you, too, will know this joy and this pain, and your sons will succeed where mine failed. It will be nothing but the greatest of honor and pleasure, so do not be afraid.

Our beloved awaits.

By The Book
Elizabeth Thorne

Catherine stared in astonishment at the naked man who had just appeared in the center of the circle she'd cast.

"Huh," she said. "I didn't actually think that would work."

Then she passed out in shock.

When she came to a few moments later, it was to the sound of fingernails tapping an impatient rhythm on the cool tile of her floor. Opening her eyes to the familiar sight of the dark brown stain on her living room ceiling, the one she always thought looked like a cupcake when she was taking a pre-dinner nap on the couch, Catherine slowly turned her head towards the noise. What she saw made her squeak and cover her face with her hands.

Apparently she hadn't imagined the whole thing. The naked man was still there, sitting in the middle of her living room. Peeking hesitantly through her fingers, she could see quite clearly that he looked… bored.

It figured, Catherine thought. She had made a fool of herself, and probably destroyed any chance of retrieving her security deposit, by actually thinking she could mystically summon love into her life using sidewalk chalk and a spell she had found in a library book. Sure, there had been an impressive puff of smoke and a man had appeared out of nowhere, but apparently the "love spell" had saddled her with a guy who was just as uninterested in her as all the ones she had met in more traditional ways.

Catherine supposed that another woman find might a modicum of encouragement in the fact that the man in question was gorgeous, naked, and in the middle of her living room, but she personally found it hard to see that as much of an improvement over all her other blind dates. True, no one had needed to pay for dinner, and the scenery was certainly nicer than usual, but it wasn't like the man was naked for her. He hadn't ended up that way because he found her beautiful and exciting and couldn't wait to ravish her in the middle of the floor. No, he was stuck with her, thanks to the intervention of powerful, irrational forces—just like her boss' younger brother had been on the dinner date that, clocking in at 3 hours, had clearly lasted at least 2 hours and 58 minutes longer than he had wanted it to.

In short, the naked man in her living room wasn't there because she was special. He was there because someone had something to hold over him.

"This was pointless," Catherine said, standing up and turning away so that she didn't embarrass either of them by staring. "I think you should go." The tapping on the floor stopped. Straightening her shoulders and trying to salvage her pride, she headed through the door and into the kitchen.

When she came back into the living room 20 minutes later with a cup of coffee, there was no sign left of the naked man's presence except for the lines of what had once been the chalk circle, which now seemed to be permanently etched into the tile floor.

"Great," Catherine said, rubbing at it with her bare toe to try and erase the marks, "I was right about the security deposit." She was standing there contemplating the potential effectiveness of various types of cleansers when the sound of a knock on her door made her jump.

Opening it, she found the naked man—only he was now wearing clothes. His attitude had also changed. Instead of looking bored, he seemed to be more than a little annoyed.

"You told me to go." Taking her open mouthed stare as an invitation, the man pushed past her, marched into the living room, and sat down on the couch. Catherine was still standing with her hand on the door, gaping at him, as he continued, "You went to all the trouble of summoning me, and then you took one look at me and told me to go. No one EVER tells me to go. Didn't you think I was handsome? Didn't you like the way I looked?"

"The way you looked? You looked naked!" Catherine realized that her voice was sounding a little shrill and tried to tone it down a bit as she closed the door to the hallway, and nervously followed him into the room. "Bored and naked," she muttered to herself unhappily.

"Yes, and?" the man asked as he picked up the cup of coffee she had been planning on drinking and finished it in one long swallow.

"Come in, why don't you. Make yourself at home." Catherine rolled her eyes as she skirted her way around the no-longer-chalk circle and took a seat in the far corner of the room where she could watch him from a safe distance.

The man stared at her, as though to say "What did you expect?" and, after a moment of impatient silence, gestured her to continue.

"Well," she glared at him, "when I saw you sitting there, I realized that I didn't really want a naked man on my floor, at least not one that got there that way... So I told you to go, and you did. Poof. Just the way you came." Catherine began tapping her fingernails on the arm of her chair, "But now you're back!" She threw her hands up in frustration. "Why *are* you back?"

When the man didn't immediately answer, Catherine took a moment to just look at him where he sat slumped on the couch, the rich red of his shirt bringing up auburn highlights in his thick brown hair. Snorting in amazement, she couldn't quite manage to keep the gloating out of her voice as she noticed something she had missed, "Are you... pouting? You *are* pouting!" All of a sudden, Catherine started to giggle. "There is a formerly naked man on my couch. Pouting."

"I am not pouting." The man on the couch glared at her in annoyance. "I've just never had anyone send me away before like that, without even saying hello, without at least trying to get to know me."

He was definitely pouting, and by that point, Catherine was laughing so hard that she could barely breathe.

"There's no need to make fun of me, you know, just because you didn't like the way I look. I may be an incubus, but I still have feelings."

Catherine put her hand over her face and tried to pull herself together. "I'm sorry," she said, "I'm sorry. I'm not laughing at you. Not really." Taking a deep breath, she put her chin in her hand and looked at him, speaking slowly and calmly as though to a kindergartener. "You are a very handsome man, and I'm sure any woman would be lucky to have you." She shrugged and let her voice return to normal. "I just really didn't expect you to show up naked like that, with a puff of smoke, in the middle of my living room."

"Oh." The pout on his face was slowly replaced by a look of interest.

"Yes," Catherine sat back in her chair with a sigh, "Oh."

The two of them sat and stared at each other in silence for a moment, before she continued, "You might as well go again. Now that you know I didn't kick you out because I found you ugly, I'm sure that you have other places you'd rather be."

"Do I have to?" The incubus sounded a little shy.

"What?"

"Do I have to go?" He dropped his curious amber eyes to his knees, "This is kind of a new situation for me, and I'd like to figure out exactly what happened."

"You actually want to stay and spend time with me?" Catherine stared in astonishment at the handsome man sitting on her couch.

"I do," he said, a blush briefly passing over his warm golden skin. "You and your accidental summoning intrigue me. In a weird way…" he paused, "In a *very* weird way, these past few hours have contained some of the most interesting events of my life."

"Let me get you another cup of coffee," Catherine squeaked, and she hurried from the room.

When she returned, a mug in each hand, the incubus was sprawled out on her couch. His head was on one arm and his feet were on the other as he stared up at the ceiling.

"It looks like a badminton birdie," he said, gesturing lazily up at the stain before sitting up to take his mug from her hand.

"I always thought it was more like a cupcake," Catherine replied offhandedly as she put the other mug down on the table and perched nervously at the far end of the couch.

The incubus took a long swallow of his drink and then looked up at the ceiling once more. "Yeah. I guess I can see that." He grinned. "So, Cupcake, do you always spend your Friday nights casting summoning spells you don't believe will work?"

Catherine blushed, "It wasn't supposed to be as summoning spell! The book said it was an invocation to welcome love into my life. I didn't expect a naked man. I expected to feel better about the fact that I was spending another Friday night at home, alone. Or possibly, I expected to feel like an idiot for wasting my time." She sighed. "At least I got the idiot part right."

"A love spell?" The incubus rolled his eyes. "No such thing."

"Wait a second," Catherine blinked at him, so surprised that she momentarily forgot to feel sorry for herself. "You, a self confessed incubus, are sitting here in my living room because I summoned you, and you're telling me that love spells don't exist?" She raised an eyebrow in consternation.

"Apples and oranges." He took another sip from his coffee. "Money, sex, these are tangible things, things you can ask for, things that demons can get you for a price. But love? Love's too big for magic. It takes time, patience, and compassion that no shortcut can provide." He smirked at her. "You are such a girl, assuming that a ritual designed to provide hot sex on demand is really a shortcut to a relationship."

"What was I supposed to think? It said it was designed to open the way to my perfect mate!"

"Cupcake, when those spells were written, they were mostly being used by men."

"So?"

"For most magicians, the perfect mate is pretty clearly defined as a creative and enthusiastic sex partner who will do anything they want and then go away again so that they can focus on their work."

"So that ritual brought you to my living room for..."

"Nothing more than a quick fuck." The incubus favored her with a lascivious grin. "Not that most women complain. I've been told that my skills in that area are," he raised his fingers in air quotes, "out of this world."

"I bet." Before she could even think about what she was doing, Catherine smacked him over the head with a throw pillow.

The next grin he sent her had nothing to do with sex, and everything to do with fun as he pulled another pillow off of the couch and hit her right back.

Soon, the fight was in full swing. Catherine made a desperate attempt to move the coffee cups to a safer place on her mantle and found herself screaming in laughter while being chased around the edges of her living room by an incubus holding a pink-tasseled, flower-printed pillow in each hand.

Finally making it back around to the couch herself, her hands relieved of their caffeinated burden, Catherine tried to ward off the demonic cheerleader by throwing a large grey seat cushion at his knees.

"En *garde!*" the incubus said, dodging her missile before tossing her one of his pillows and going into a classic fencing stance.

Catherine marveled for a moment as his ability to look dashing while wielding such a ridiculous weapon, and then mirrored his position. "*Touché?*" she asked. Then, raising her pillow over her head, she set to.

Ten minutes later, the two combatants were lying on the floor, out of breath and exhausted from laughter. They were still half heartedly swatting at each other's heads from an arm's distance away when the incubus suddenly rolled over and pinned Catherine to the ground.

"I surrender!" she laughed, "I surrender!" and then gasped in astonishment as, instead of pummeling her further with his trusty throw pillow, he kissed her.

The incubus' lips were soft on hers and his hair, where it fell against her face, smelled like cinnamon and myrrh. Deciding it was hard to be self conscious with anyone you had just fought to a draw in an epic pillow battle, she pushed her fingers through its soft strands and kissed him back.

For a while they just lay together on the ground kissing, nibbling on each other's lips, and smiling. Then, for no apparent reason, the incubus pulled back.

Catherine opened her eyes to see his warm amber eyes looking down at her and a question on his face

"Are you okay with this?" he asked.

"Do I not seem okay with it?" Catherine pushed herself up to her elbows and tried not to wonder whether the question was some sort of comment on her technique.

"You do, but," the incubus looked to the side, no longer meeting her eyes, "when we could have done this earlier, you sent me away."

"Oh for goodness sake." Catherine could not fail to recognize the irony in the situation. She had sent him away because she had assumed he didn't want her. Now he was withdrawing because he thought that she didn't want him.

"I vanished you," she took a moment to dwell on the ridiculousness of that statement, *I vanished you?* "because I thought you didn't want to be here. I didn't want to be just another man's obligation. It's different now. You want to be here." Suddenly she was once again the insecure one, "I think."

The incubus looked back at her and grinned, "Do you think I engage in furniture warfare with just anyone?" When Catherine didn't immediately reply, he said quietly, "I chose to kiss you. That's not part of my standard repertoire."

"Why did you?" she asked shyly.

"Because we were having fun, and I liked you." He smiled at her. "I like you."

Catherine could not resist smiling back. "I like you too."

With the sound of that affirmation in his ears, the incubus kissed her again. This time his lips were more demanding, and the intensity of his focus on her made Catherine moan and fist her hands in his hair. Through the thin fabric of her silk pajamas she could feel the incubus growing larger inside his jeans, and she tilted her hips so that he would rub up against her where she needed him most.

For a moment, the incubus ground against Catherine, giving her what she wanted. Then he pulled his lips away to kneel above her, his weight holding her hips to the floor. Quickly unbuttoning his brick red shirt, he threw it aside. Catherine, however, had only a moment to appreciate the phenomenal view of his muscular, bronze chest, before he reached down, ran his long fingers along the sides of her rib cage until they reached the hem of her camisole, and drew it slowly up over her head.

"Lovely," he grinned. "Like pillows." Catherine briefly swatted at him before gasping as he took the weight of her breasts in his hands, and gently began stroking the undersides with his fingers. A look of intense concentration crossed his face, and he smiled as he gently squeezed and then caressed the skin, coming tantalizingly close to her sensitive nipples but not quite touching them.

"Tease," Catherine tried to shift under his hands to move the contact where she wanted it. The incubus, however, continued to smile and taunt her with his fingers for long, agonizing moments before suddenly lowering himself on top of her to take one of her nipples into his warm, wet mouth.

Catherine moaned, digging her fingers into the muscles of his shoulders in pleasure at the deep sucking sensations he focused on her breast. His hands continued to play across her skin, squeezing her other nipple firmly and then replacing the strength of his fingers with the gentle rasp of his tongue.

Running her hands down along the incubus' back, Catherine grabbed the firm globes of his ass and trying to drag his pelvis back up towards where she wanted it against hers. The incubus, however, was immovable. He simply looked up at her for a moment and grinned before bringing his attention back to her breasts.

Two can play at that game, Catherine thought, and moved her hands around to the front of his body so that she could touch him through his jeans. His teeth tightened momentarily on her nipple as her hand stroked his turgid cock through the material, and he lifted his hips off hers for long enough that she could unbuckle his pants and set him free.

Catherine stroked the silky skin of his cock gently before beginning to work the long, thick shaft with both her hands. The thought of having that firm rod inside her made so excited that her legs separated as though of their own accord.

The incubus took her movement as an invitation and suddenly his hand was between her legs. The sensation made Catherine throw back her head in pleasure as he grinned, "You're so wet you've soaked through your pajama bottoms."

Blushing at his words, Catherine turned her head away, her hands stilling on his cock as he continued to use his fingers to caress her through the thin, damp fabric.

"No," the incubus said, "I like it." Raising his hand to his mouth, he licked his finger tips, "You taste like the ocean." Then, holding her eyes, he gently pulled back from her grip, slowly drew the silk pants over her hips, and tossed them aside.

Catherine tensed in nervousness as he knelt down between her legs. The movement felt too intimate, but his warm, amber eyes were encouraging and full of desire as he separated her curls with his fingers and slowly lowered his head to her mound. His long, pointed tongue flicked out once against her clitoris to make her gasp, and then dipped lower, tasting her and swirling briefly around the entrance to her body before sliding up along her inner lips.

Holding her open with his fingers, the incubus continued to tease her with his lips and tongue until the sensations were almost too overpowering to take. When Catherine started to push him away, he held her wrists to the bed so that he could continue his pleasurable assault. Alternating gently sucking and nibbling at her clitoris with long intimate strokes of his tongue, the gentle restraint allowed Catherine to relax into the feelings he caused in her until she fell, gasping, over the edge to orgasm.

When she got her breath back, the incubus was still kneeling between her legs, gently stroking her with his fingers. "More?" he asked, suddenly slipping two of them inside her and hooking them up against her g-spot to make her jump.

"How long," Catherine tried desperately to keep control of her voice as his fingers gently stroked inside her and his thumb began to tickle her clit, "are you going to make me wait before you fuck me?"

"Well," he grinned, "I guess if you're that eager..."

Pulling his fingers slowly out of her, the incubus rubbed the fluids they had gathered down the length of his arousal. Watching him handle his cock only increased Catherine's excitement, and she whimpered in longing as he rubbed the head slowly over her clit to tease her a bit more before finally finding his angle and beginning to push inside.

The incubus was generously built, and Catherine gasped at the intensity of the sensation as, inch by inch, the demon worked himself into her—pulling back, pushing forward, and circling his hips to try and make himself room. It took long, glorious, minutes of erotic encouragement before he managed to lodge the full length and breadth of his cock inside of her, and she enjoyed every one of them. The stretching sensation was a pleasure so intense that it bordered on pain, and she cried out in ecstasy as he filled her in a way she had never imagined. When his hips were finally snug up tight against hers, the incubus rested deep in her body for a moment before taking one of her legs, lifting it up to his shoulder, and beginning to move.

Slow, dragging thrusts quickly brought Catherine to the brink of orgasm once more. The incubus kept her there, smiling, for what felt like hours, until she writhed and begged underneath him. Then, with one final push of his hips and a flick of his thumb over her most sensitive spot, he bottomed out against her cervix and sent them both over the edge.

When they were both able to move again, the incubus rolled over onto his back and pulled Catherine into the hollow of his chest. She was just beginning to snuggle in comfortably when he tensed under her and suddenly said, "I shouldn't be here."

"What?" Catherine suddenly felt like she was about to cry. "I can't believe this. Even a sex demon wants nothing to do with me." She started crawling away to look for her clothing, mortified by what she'd just done.

The demon in question grabbed her ankle and yanked her attention back towards him. "Don't be ridiculous, woman. I'm perfectly happy to be there" he made a lewd gesture at her lower body. "I just shouldn't be able to be HERE!" With that exclamation, he pointed at the lines of the circle, which he had ended up sprawled across at the climax of their passion.

Catherine shook her head in confusion. "I don't understand."

The incubus looked at Catherine in a way that made her feel like she was the slowest student in class. "Any power circle strong enough to summon me should also hurt like hell any time I try to cross it—even from the wrong side." He tentatively poked at the patterns on which they lay. "Yet, somehow I just rolled on top of this thing without even feeling a twinge. That makes absolutely no sense."

"I know." Still feeling somewhat mortified, Catherine tried to hide behind her hair. "This whole thing is completely insane."

"No." The demon grabbed her chin, and the look on his face was frighteningly intense. "I mean this *really* makes no sense." Rolling to his feet, he stood up, and started stalking around the edges of the circle.

Catherine watched him pace, discomfort slowly abandoned to amazement at how completely comfortable the incubus was in his skin. He was, she thought, still capable of looking gorgeous with that screwed-up, worried expression on his face... and that made her slowly start to believe that his concern might actually have nothing to do with her at all.

"Show me the book," he demanded suddenly.

"What?" Catherine tried to stop focusing on his perfectly round ass and start listening to his words.

"The book. The book with the summoning spell." The incubus stopped pacing and turned the full intensity of his gaze on her. "I need to see what you did."

"Okay..." Catherine pulled the throw from the couch and wrapped it around her shoulders as she went to search for the volume. It took a few minutes of tossing around pillow fight detritus, but eventually she found the ancient hardcover in the far corner of the room. Opening it up to the correct page, she handed the spell to him.

The demon looked at the book, looked back at the circle, checked the book once again, and then kicked at the line on the floor—stubbing his toe on the tile and hopping around for a moment in pain.

"This shouldn't have worked." He waved the volume at Catherine as though to imply that was somehow her fault.

"Don't look at me! You're the one who's supposed to know about magic, Mister 'I get summoned for sex all the time and the ladies think it's out of this world.'"

"I do know about magic," He slammed the book to the floor, grabbed her shoulders, and turned her to look at the circle. "And I'm telling you this shouldn't have worked. It's not a proper summoning spell at all! It looks like someone crossed a hex designed to wither your neighbor's crops with a bunch of fertility symbols and glued it all together with a nursery rhyme. This circle shouldn't have been able to call a mouse out of its hole if you filled it with cheese. It shouldn't have done anything at all!"

"Um." Catherine gently disengaged her fingers from her shoulders and picked up the library book to put it on the coffee table. "Forgive me for pointing out the obvious, but it did work. It summoned you. I drew the circle, recited the spell, turned around three times, and 'poof' I had a naked man on my floor... along with enough damage to my tile to make my landlord want to lock me up and throw away the key."

"Turned around..." The incubus was staring at her as though she had grown a second head.

"Don't look at me like that. I thought that was how magic worked! And it did!" Gesturing to the relevant items, she continued, "I summoned you with *that* circle and *that* spell. Then I realized I didn't want any man who was only in my apartment because he was forced to be there, so I told you to go and you did!" She poked him in the chest with her finger. "But then you came back."

"I was curious!" He backed up.

Catherine harrumphed in disbelief and poked him again.

"Alright. I was annoyed and curious."

"Getting closer." Another poke, and the demon landed on the couch.

"You rejected me, and that's never happened before. I wanted to find out why." He shrugged his shoulders. "Sure, a lot of it was that you hurt my feelings, but do you know how rarely something happens that I don't expect? Do you have any idea how exciting novelty is when you've been alive for centuries?"

"It figures," Catherine shook her head and looked away. "Even immortal demons think I'm strange."

The incubus growled with frustration. "You're interesting. You interested me. You interest me."

"Really?"

"I've never felt quite like this before." The incubus reached out to grab Catherine's hands and pulled her into his lap.

"Like what?"

"Fascinated... frustrated... like I care." He sighed and rested his chin on her head. "It's weird."

"You're telling me." She snuggled closer as he petted her hair, and together they stared out at the mess they had made of her living room.

"What happens next?" Catherine eventually asked, careful not to look him in the eye.

"I don't know, Cupcake. I've never stuck around this long before." She felt him shrug behind her. "We clean up, I guess, and then have dinner."

Turning to him in surprise, she asked "You're staying?"

"If you don't mind," he smiled. "I'd kind of like to see how this plays out."

Catherine grinned at the incubus, and he hugged her briefly to him before they both stood up and started putting on their clothes.

They had almost finished straightening up the room when the incubus paused once again at the edge of the circle's etched black lines. "I stand by my statement that there's no magic that can shorten the journey it takes to make somebody love you," he said, weighing the throw pillow he held in his hands. "But I'm beginning to wonder if maybe, just maybe, sometimes the universe is willing to take a few unorthodox shortcuts when steering two people into each other's arms."

Catherine had less than a second to stare at him in amazement before the flowered accessory hit her smack in the face.

Outermost Claw, Front Right Foot
Steven Schwartz

I am Outermost Claw, Front Right Foot, and I am content in my life, though almost no one who knew me before would believe it.

They would still try and call me Belinda, daughter of Galliard and Beatrice, Lord and Lady Mistral. And it is true, that was once my name, and my role. But they do not understand what, and why, I am what I am now. They have not rubbed themselves, open-legged, against its hard pearlescent surface, or had their breath catch as the point quivered inside them as their lover trembled in its sleep. I do not know of what my wondrous Charyon dreams—I suspect I would know as little of its dreams as a field mouse of mine—but it delights me that it does, even as it scares me when the sharp, sharp point, made to poke holes in the armor of a knight, or a rhinoceros, or cleave stone, pushes against me as I cradle it between my breasts. I bear the scars of the dragon's dreams, but its claw is made brighter and more lustrous by my juices as I rub against it, as I lick it clean, as I strive to polish and protect it.

My life may be shorter than many—Right Eye and Left Eye, Wing-Joint and Anus, the Phallus Siblings—but that does not make it any less full; we are all the lovers of Charyon, and it is around its splendor that we make our lives.

The life I have now, spending my days tending to a dragon's claw, is not the one that I expected as I grew up. Service was something that others gave to me, even though my father was but a minor member of the gentry of the land. I had a nursemaid, then a lady's maid and a governess, and a tutor, and a chaperone, until the day it changed.

❖

The chaperone had but recently come into my life, I having just turned of age. She was the sort of woman who believed that as she was not enjoying herself, no one else should, and that the mere presence of a man near me was enough to put me at grave risk of Forgetting Myself. I would tell you more about her, but the years since I've known her have wiped all but those few impressions from me; her name, a burst of meaningless syllables (like Belinda), is long gone. Here, under the high mountain, names that mean nothing vanish.

There was no risk of that on the day things changed, as my father burst in to the room in which I was being educated, sitting close to the fire with my tutor. Behind him were four armed and armored men, in the red-and-blue livery of the Earl, my father's liege lord.

When the chaperone stood to protest, her words were cut off by a jerk of my father's hand. "Belinda; you are going with these men." His voice was brusque, cold, and far too rapid for his usual speech.

"Now, father? But I'm...." Those were the last words I was to say to him, and he cut me off as harshly as he would the head of some foe in battle.

"You will go. Now. The King has commanded our lord to appease Charyon, and you are that appeasement."

Silly me, not knowing then what I know now—I dropped to the floor and screamed, so hard and so long that the world turned grey, and then it slipped away from me in the dark.

We each take turns, climbing up from our beds of gold, or tattered tapestries, or the parts of our beloved flat enough to hold us as we sleep, and go to take watch. Not many people try to disturb a dragon, but those who do are worth knowing about before they arrive; they are either crazy, very skilled, or both, and can cause trouble for us.

Perhaps if I had gone out that day, instead of looking plaintively at Left Eye, who could not sleep with his beloved part (for Charyon rested its head on the left side that night), things would have been different. But I was so happy, head nestled against the knuckle of its outermost toe, on the right, so close to the claw—I could not bring myself to be torn away.

So it was that Left Eye rose up, and went to keep an eye on the pass leading up to our mountain, and came back an hour later, calling all of us to arms. "Many of them, with carts and pikes and armor!"

So warned, I rolled off the toe, wincing as my most recent scar from my beloved Claw (Charyon had twitched while I was near it, and the cut ran down my arm; I had licked the point clean of my blood, delighting in the contact) and put on my armor, and grabbed my weapon; I was, as always, to go to the front.

Some of us had weapons salvaged from our attackers, or collected in some raid Charyon had gone on years before, but mine were special. Every few years, the Claw that I loved so would split, old covering coming off like a cat's claw, replaced by the new. I gathered those pieces up, and made of them plates of armor, a helmet, a long curved blade; I armored myself with my beloved, and charged into battle for it.

At least, I thought as I surveyed my condition when I awoke, they left me my dignity. While not finely dressed (what point was there, after all, in wasting finery on someone about to be a meal), I was dressed, and the cords that bound me to the rock were not too tight; I suppose they did not wish to risk me hurting myself and displeasing the dragon with the condition I was in.

I had first awoken in darkness, the feel of fabric on my skin telling me I was hooded, the sounds of birds and the warmth of sun on my skin telling me it was still daytime. After a few deep breaths, I started to gather my wits to speak; perhaps there was still something I could say to save my life, I thought. Something I could offer these men, even if one of them was my father, to avoid the fate I was headed to.

But I must have shifted, or done something to give myself away, because the next thing I knew I was smelling something strong, and awareness slipped away once more.

And I awoke bound to the rock, waiting for the dragon. But they had left me with my eyes open, and my mind clear.

I heard it before I felt it, and felt it before I saw it; the concussive thud of its massive beating wing, then the wind as it drew closer. When the dragon landed in the clearing in front of me, it might as well have been night—the wings and body so large they blotted out the sun.

I kept my eyes on it, though, not wanting to look away; both because it would have been undignified, and because what I could see, half-shadowed as it was, and my eyes still adjusting to the vanished sun—was beautiful. The curve of wings powerful enough to lift that massive form into the air was a curve more perfect than any I'd seen before, whether in the arch of a flying buttress or the shape of the breasts I'd admired when my friends and I had bathed. There was never hair as flowing or iridescent as the scales along the dragon's neck, and never jewelry more beautiful than the claws and teeth that reached for me.

And the eye—for it was the eye that met mine (Charyon's head was far too massive at this close range for me to see both at once—the eye I could lose myself in (and later, I would try, only to have the woman who was Right Eye and the man who was Left Eye explain to me the error of my ways, with their words, their fists, and their feet) regarded me, and though I could feel the hot breath of the dragon leeching the moisture from my skin, making it impossible for me to cry even if I wanted to, I did not look away.

But in that moment, I wanted Charyon to do with me as it would; I knew that though I could never be nourishment to something so large, so ancient, so powerful, I might be an amusee-bouche, a morsel of delectation; or might serve some other purpose—any other purpose.

The claw that the dragon brought forward was the outermost,

on the right front foot; and I strained forward to meet it, tugging against my bonds. There was no point in shying away, even if I had wanted to; the difference between freedom and disembowelment was not going to be made by my actions.

The claw started just above the first rope, and sliced through the dress I was wearing and, from the pain I could feel, some of my skin, but I did not pull back, and I did not look away. As it slid down, the pain did not stop, but each loop of rope it cut set me freer, let me lean against it (I could feel the warmth of my own blood as I lay forward) and when the last rope left, and I collapsed against that claw, I found release, my body shaking in the orgasm that had wrapped itself in all the tension and fear and pain.

And when the claws closed so gently around me, even though they scarred me and turned the garment I'd worn into ribbons, I did not faint; as Charyon carried me back to its lair, I did not even close my eyes.

I charged up the steep incline from my beloved's nest to the entrance, a trip I had made hundreds of times, and burst out into the open air. Almost at once I could tell something was wrong, something was different. When people came to slay the dragon, they came with mighty weapons of war, or armor so thick they could barely move in it. One clever soul came with a way to run water over his armor as he ventured in, for fear of the dragon's breath. I was impressed, even as I slipped the scimitar I'd made from my beloved claw between two plates of armor and up to his heart.

But this was a rabble—a large rabble, it's true, and for such a thing well-armored; but how they expected to bring down a dragon, any dragon, let alone my mighty beloved, who could burn a galleon with a breath, or shear a house from its foundations with a swoop of one clawed foot, with pikes and iron helms was beyond me.

I could see them flinch and stare as I emerged, not the dragon they were looking for, but a wild maiden leading other wild ones;

naked save for the pearlescent curved armor that I wore, crying out my beloved's name as a battle cry.

Three of them fell before me, learning that iron armor was no match for a claw splintered off from a dragon's toe—I could feel my beloved's mind touching mine, delighting in the spray of blood, in the delicate movements as I danced from one foe to the next, in the arc of my sword strike that was a tribute and pale imitation of Charyon's own blows.

Then I heard a cry, a cry of a name I'd not answered to in a decade—"Belinda!" and my attention was torn away, and the tendril of my beloved's mind left me. Ahead of me, standing in a gap between two high rocks, a narrow point through which either they or I would have to pass, was a knight—or at least someone in knight's armor, for the voice I heard was higher than I expected of a knight old enough to wear so much plate.

I did not want to be reminded of who I'd been—that world had left me behind, and while I owed it thanks that I was now with my beloved, that was no reason to give it quarter, or respect, or anything beyond the sharp point of my sword. I charged, screaming out Charyon's name...

...and the nets came down from the rocks above me, and the stones almost immediately thereafter; for while I sliced through two nets, once my hand was hit and my sword was lost from it, I was trapped. Then, I felt the sting of darts hitting my flesh, bare where the armor did not cover it. And, just as I had before, I faded into darkness.

I had not expected to be in company when Charyon set me down on the floor of its cave, still bloodied and shaking. But the men and women there welcomed me, telling me their names and bathing and binding my wounds. They were all naked, or adorned only in the jewels of the hoard, like paintings framed in gold and gems; for our beloved did not wear clothes, and its heat was more than ample to keep us warm; why should we have anything between us and it, when we did not need to?

The rules were explained to me—how one did not approach another's part of the body without permission, how we addressed each other, how we took shifts on watch; there were not many other rules.

Instead, there were the strange ways our new world was different.

"What are those?" I asked Anus, pointing to ovoids, wrapped in tapestries or finery, off to one side. "Those are our predecessors, sleeping the sleep of Charyon, playing in his dreams. Perhaps, so I've heard, one day they may hatch as his eggs."

I started to laugh, but I felt the weight of Charyon's mind upon me when I drew in breath; he had picked me out as a lighthouse lantern might, sweeping across a still ocean. And while I did not know what Anus had said to be true, I knew it was important enough not to mock.

"Does it... speak to you?" Anus asked me, his hand on my shoulder. "I recognize that look."

"Not with words, but...." Then I paused. "It? Why would you not call him he?" For I had seen, as Charyon laid on one side, the Phallus siblings tending to their charge, stroking their bodies along its glistening shaft, using their tongues and their own juices to add to its sheen, to make it quiver beneath them as they laid upon it.

And Anus laughed, and led me further down the body; and there, between his charge and the phallus, there was a slit so fine I could barely see it, and would have walked right by had I not seen five curled toes just barely poking out. "She's inside; that's a position that's never empty for long, though all we ever see is the barest fragment."

"But does she not come out to eat? Or does Charyon provide nourishment?" I had not yet truly begun to think of my beloved by that title; and I could not yet bring myself to call that magnificent creature "it."

The moment after I asked the question, I blushed; for I had not been thinking of whom I'd asked it, and was afraid I would embarrass him. But he shook his head. "None of us need to eat; I think the magic of our lord fills us with all we need. All we need do is enjoy it, and serve it as we would."

That said, he returned to his charge, nestling in it and looking for all the world like a fairy in a flower in some children's book.

I awoke sore; but not the fulfilling soreness of a new scar from my beloved claw, or the pleasant reminding soreness after a night of abandon with Charyon's other lovers. This was the soreness of bruises from blows, the drunkenness of drugs not taken of one's own free will.

Unlike the last time I'd woken up somewhere not of my free will (drugged or otherwise), I was unbound. I was also undressed, though I could feel the fabric of bandages on my arms. Looking around, once my sight had cleared enough to do so, revealed a four-post bed, curtains drawn on all sides; a moment's privacy, at least, while I gathered my thoughts.

Down pillows, though, were not as comfortable as gold coins, when my beloved was not there. I could not even feel him in the most distant corners of my mind, could not feel the once-a-minute beating of his heart.

Instead, I heard the clank of metal on stone; it sounded like armor hitting the floor, and, by rolling over and peeking out past the curtains, I was able to determine the truth of that.

The warrior who'd challenged me was sitting by the window, looking out, short hair all I could see of the face. Scattered on the floor were plates of armor—pauldron, coulter, and vambrace, leaving bare arms, the curaiss on the bench in front, leaving only the padded undergarment; the warrior still had on cuisses and greaves, legs still in gleaming metal that reminded me (especially the pointed tips of the sabatons covering his feet) for a moment of my lost beloved.

Then the warrior sighed, and pulled at the laces holding the upper padding on with surprisingly delicate hands. When that too slipped away, I was shocked; more shocked than I had been when first I saw toes poking out of my beloved. The warrior's breasts, while not so beautifully curved as, say, Wingtip Joint's (and the memory of fondling them as we both sat cushioned in Charyon's wing, her hands on the joint as I played with her, was more painful than the bruises I could still feel) were clearly those of a woman, and the voice I'd heard stirred memories that I was fumbling to recover; fumbling, until she heard my gasp of surprise, and turned to me.

I could not remember her name, still; but the face of the stern chaperone that had challenged my father the day I was taken— that I had not forgotten, and even shorn of her locks, baring a scar or two not unlike my own, I knew her, and saw in her eyes a love I'd not seen directed at me for years.

"Belinda... you're awake."

I could only nod; hearing that name that used to be mine was as confusing, as befuddling, as anything they had put on the darts.

"You remember me, yes?" And again, all I could do was nod, and continue watching her as she undid the buckles and fastenings of her remaining armor. "We rescued several others, but it was you I was praying to see."

"Me? But why? Did my family...." She snorted, and a mask of contempt drew itself across her face, making the scars ugly, instead of the beauty I'd seen in them just a moment ago.

"They were content to let you go. I left them, for I'd no charge left, and no one there knew how much I'd loved you." Her anger was accentuated by the clatter of metal on stone, but now she was free of it, and pulled the long woolen trousers down; now she and I were of a kind, naked, scarred, and unsure of ourselves; or at least I fancied I saw some hint of uncertainty in her gait as she moved to the bed. "I'm not sure even you did."

I wanted to rage at her; I wanted to throw her out of the bed and demand to be taken back home, back to Charyon, but I knew it would be futile; even if she was now unarmored, the men she had brought with her had weapons, and I had nothing. And when she touched me, touched my face with her hand, I let slip the hope that I would see my lighthouse again; and now, a small boat adrift in a storm, I was prepared to find shelter where I could.

That she had guarded me once before helped; that once before I'd been left on a rock to face my fate alone, only to have a lover deliver themselves to me made it simpler, I suppose, and I am not, nor have I ever been, truly a warrior; I fought only in the frenzy of defending love. Now, my love was far away, and someone else claimed they loved me.

That she was scarred made it easier; her fingers could run down the hardened skin between my breasts without question, without disgust. I could look at her and see some fragment of myself reflected. We had both been scarred by our love, and in that way, we understood each other.

We did not kiss; I had never kissed a love upon the mouth (how can you, when that mouth is longer than you are tall, and belongs to two others?), but I did open my arms to her as she climbed in the bed.

I think she would have kissed me, had I not moved my mouth away; but there was so much more, it seemed, she wanted to do with that mouth. Between repeating my name (and now, embarrassment, a feeling I thought I'd forgotten long ago, was beginning to creep back in, that I had forgotten hers) and kissing what else she could (my collarbone, my shoulder, my neck), her mouth was busy, as were her hands, tracing the scars along my body.

At first, I was at a loss what to do.

I had heard the sounds of lovemaking from the first day I arrived; but, in my foolishness, I ascribed them to people not sufficiently in love with our wondrous beloved—people who could not find the spines on its back as fulfilling as I found my claw.

This delusion lasted for a week; until Charyon rolled over (and I heard for the first time the ancient voice in my head, speaking a word I did not know, but could understand as Flee!—which I did, along with all my fellows not too enclosed in its body or asleep) and the claw was now under its enormous serpentine bulk.

I tried to bond with another claw, that had no lover—there were many, after all, so why could I not choose? But it was not the same. Oh, I could still rub against it, still make my nipples erect from rubbing against its milky surface—but it was swimming towards an ever-receding shore. These claws were not my claws, and my claw was away from my reach. I sat down on a divan of a fashion I did not recognize, plundered no doubt from a city I'd never heard of.

Right Eye, who was in the same condition, came and put a hand on my shoulder. "It becomes easier; this is the first time you've been without, no?"

I nodded, too tired from my exertions to speak.

"Some people try and dig under the hoard to make their way; the lucky ones give up before the hoard shifts, and traps them."

The thought had not even occurred to me, and for a moment I was furious with myself for not having thought of it. But I was no engineer, no excavator, and what would happen to my beloved and the claw if I were to be trapped?

Right Eye sat down next to me, his thigh against mine, and his hands touched the nipples that showed to the world both my excitement and my frustration. It was a good touch, even if it was not what I wanted. "Let us comfort each other, while we wait for Charyon to roll again."

And my foolish superiority drained away; now I understood the sounds I'd heard, now I understood that these were not people insufficient in their love, but people unable to reach their love; and our mighty beloved could not be jealous of us together—it would be like my being jealous of a hairbrush laid too close to a comb by my old mirror, both of them ready to hand, and eager to caress my hair.

"I must warn you, Right Eye, before I came here I'd never known the touch of man, and still have never done so—not until now."

He laughed. "Then I'll be gentle with you, and teach you

what I can."

To one accustomed to a lover sharp, hard, and ungiving, a man came as a strange surprise; I pressed against him and he moved; I could feel the muscles in his arms giving way as I sunk my fingers into them.

And he was cooler—for the blood that runs in a dragon's claw is still dragon's blood, and far warmer than any we have inside us. I could kiss his skin and not feel thirsty for a cool drink.

I do not know how long we spent on that couch; in the presence of a dragon, for whom thirty years can be a nap, time does not seem to matter. I know that I joked that his claws were not so sharp as my beloved's, but having them inside me did feel good, and he curved them, making them even more clawlike; and I felt a release akin, though not as grand, as that I felt with my beloved.

And I asked him, as I could not ask Charyon, what he would like me to do for him. I was not surprised, but I was pleased, that many of the things he asked of me were things I had done, or tried to do, with the claw. His seed was salty, like my own blood when the claw had cut my tongue, and it was a wonderful reminder, and I drank it greedily. I looked at him, and he at me, and we could see our beloved reflected in each other's bodies.

After that first time, though I still burned for the love of my claw, I could gain some cool relief in the skins of my fellows, and they in mine. We understood each other, and grew to understand more. The way Right Eye had looked at me, never closing his eyes no matter what we did, made more sense after I realized that Anus preferred mine to place his prick, no matter what else might be available; and when I realized that I had left a fine tracery of nailmarks on his back while we fucked, that I saw only when he slept afterwards.

After that night, after I saw the beads of dried blood on his back, then I knew I could truly be called Outermost Claw, Right Front Foot. The next day, when Charyon rolled back, the first discarded splinter of claw was left behind, and I began to fashion my weapon.

Though she did not share my beloved, as Right Eye did, still she had been without that which she loved for so long that it would be cruel of me, now, to deny her; or to resist taking the pleasure that I could in her, with my own beloved so far away, no matter on which side it rested.

And so, as her fingers tracing my scars led her down between my legs, I opened them for her; and learning from the way she kissed me, I kissed her skin in return, enjoying once more the delicious cool skin, made saltier by the sweat still there from her time in armor. I drew her nipple into my mouth, and listened as she called my name again and again as I sucked at it, licked at it— I thought of biting it but no matter how hardened and strong she had been in her armor, she was no dragon.

Then it was time for me to return her calls, though my own were wordless; she had learned, though I must assume from some other source, how to curve her fingers inside me, how to let her thumb land at my most sensitive spot, how to make me lose my attention, my attachment to the world...

...and from the grunt of pain she made, I had not lost my sharp nails, and even now, so far away, was true to my claw in that aspect.

Later, I would return the favor, careful with my own fingertips (I knew, when I paid attention, how sharp they were, and I did not want to hurt her; she had not had time and sharpness to build up resistance as I had, deep inside me.

Even away from the dragon, time seemed to vanish; I could not count hours, and though it was light outside when we started, I know it was dark when I drifted off to sleep, trying as best I could to stretch out and still rest as much of my skin as I could against the little finger of her right hand.

I woke before she did, though it was by only a matter of seconds. I think that I heard something in my head, even before I felt the faintest hint of a much stronger gust of wind. A flicker of heat against my outstretched left foot, closest to the window.

Then the screams and cries started, and my chaperone awoke with a start, nearly flinging me off. And below the screams—a crackle, and a low, resounding, beat; a beat of wind far lower in pitch than any gong could make.

We pushed aside the curtains, and there was no doubt as to what was happening; the flickering light from outside was not that of a single torch, or even a few dozen—it was the burning of a wooden roof.

"Help me, Belinda!" As my chaperone—was she now my lover? I wasn't sure—raced for her padded garments, and her armor scattered about the floor. I listened to her instruction, though my mind was racing down other paths—was the fire an accident? A coincidence? I couldn't help but hope as I helped her step into the padded trousers, reached for the undercoat....

And my questions were answered by the sounds of snapping tiles and the groans of snapping timbers, just before a buffet of wind knocked me to the ground. The roof was gone, though I could hardly see any more stars than I had when it was there—my beloved's wings blotted them out. I dropped the coat, staggered to my feet, and moved to the center of the room, better to be seen. It had come for me, I was certain; and I did not care whether it was love that brought it, or wounded pride, or boredom; the motivations of a mind far older and greater than mine were not things I would understand.

My chaperone plucked her sword from the floor, and raced towards me, trying to move between me and the right front foot, that even now reached down through the shattered roof. I could see that the effort of breaking that tile and wood had hurt the claw on the outside, which might already have been close to splitting; I saw it and wanted it again.

My chaperone's sword hit the second innermost claw, and it was a fine weapon—I could see it made a significant divot, not enough to threaten the quick inside, but more than most weapons could have made—and then the outermost claw closed around me, and I saw Charyon's head slithering down towards us.

Was it going to eat me now? Or welcome me back? I had no idea, and waited, delighted just to be back, even as I felt the edges of the claw break my skin once more.

Aside from feeling his mind wash past me, though, his head did not stop—and his right eye fixed, intently, on my chaperone; she brought her blade up to take a swing at it, and I could almost hear Right Eye crying out in anguish back at the mountain.

But at the apex of her two-handed swing, sword poised above her head, she met the dragon's gaze. The sword remained there, held above her head, her arms quivering with the effort, as Charyon reached back down, and using the second innermost claw, the one she'd struck, it plucked her from the floor as well, as stiff as a statue, unable—or unwilling—to move.

And we flew away, we three, leaving behind the burning houses, the ruined manor's roof, and the horrified and furious mob behind us.

There have been no alarms these past—how long has it been? I do not know. Time does not matter as much in the dragon's cave.

And time matters even less when, with a great stretch, I can reach my arm out, and just brush with my fingertips the fingertips of my dear Second Innermost Claw, as we both balance, holding the claws beneath us between our legs, rubbing gently against them. When Charyon rolls, we will lie together—but for now its front right foot is above the hoard, open to the magical air, and we could not be happier.

(October 30, 1938)

Frank came charging into the living room much like a bull in the proverbial china shop, knocking over my prized Tiffany lamp in the process. The crash of glass startled me out of my stupor, my heart pounding wildly. I had been listening to the music hour on the radio, gently falling into slumber, my darning untouched in my lap. I thought about reprimanding Frank in the strongest possible way, but then I saw the fear on his face. Frank had taken on a deathly shade of white, as if all the blood had drained from his body. At first, I seriously thought someone had shot him, or he had come off worse in an altercation with a piece of farm machinery. Frank had recently purchased one of them combine machines. Yet I could see no evidence of blood and consequently no rational explanation for his brutish behaviour. I mean, to burst into your neighbours house on a quiet Sunday evening to frighten the life out of her! Truth be told, Frank and I were more than friendly neighbours. Ever since his wife Maureen died last winter, we had drawn close. Closer than any God-fearing neighbour had a right to be. Thou shall not covet thy neighbor's wife—the writing in the Bible for anyone to read. So Frank and I skirted the edge of temptation without ever crossing the line. Although we had grown accustomed to spending the occasional evening together, since my dear husband Jack plied his trade on the road. But Frank had never ventured into the house uninvited before. Never!

For a moment, Frank just stood there—dumb as a mule— breathing hard while trying to say something. "What on earth's going on, Frank? Why did you burst in like that?" I had a sudden premonition that perhaps something horrible had happened to Jack. Perhaps he had had an automobile accident on the way to Birmingham. Though, if he had, wouldn't the police have informed me? I waited patiently for Frank to offer me an explanation. He tried hard to draw breath so he could answer. I calculated that he must have run a long way to get so out of breath. Frank is a farmer, so he wasn't adverse to hard labour and was as

Invasion!
Beverly Langland

fit as any man his age. He probably cut across the fields, judging by the state of his boots. He had left a muddy trail right back to the kitchen door. I grew impatient for an answer, and Frank could obviously tell from the look on my face. After one big intake of breath, he finally spoke. "Martha," he said. "Get Jack's gun!"

Frank looked as earnest as I have ever seen him. "Whatever for?"

"Do as you're told, woman."

Special relationship or not, I felt incensed. "Now listen here, Frank Johnson. You have no right to speak to me that way!" Even Jack, who had a sour reputation of growing angry at the slightest provocation, had never raised his voice to me. Never, in all the years we had been married. I stood firm, crossing my arms across my chest, demanding an explanation. I even came close to stamping my foot.

"Do you trust me, Martha?"

"Why, of course Frank, but—"

"Then get the gun and put on some warm clothes."

"Frank—"

"Please. For me. I'll explain later."

Frank remained solemn, so I took him on faith. I collected Jack's shotgun and cartridges from the cupboard in the kitchen and handed the weapon to Frank, who I found busy gathering the pieces of my broken lamp. Then I went upstairs to change into warmer clothing. When I came back, Frank had retuned the radio station to CBS. He had the volume low, so he had his ear pressed against the speaker. When he noticed me, he hurriedly turned the set off. "Sorry," he said. "I didn't want to frighten you."

"But you are frightening me, Frank. In God's name, what's going on?"

"I'll explain in the pickup."

"Are we going somewhere?"

"Yes."

"Where?"

"Anywhere away from here."

By here, did he mean the farm or Knox County? I had by then realized something serious had happened. Frank handed me Jack's shotgun and I followed him across the muddy fields, back to his farmhouse, my mind racing with each step. Not so long ago, there had been talk of a Russian invasion, or the Germans or the Japanese. I didn't take much heed of the foreign news. We had our own problems here at home. Yet, if someone had invaded, how could they reach Tennessee so quickly without our defenses spotting them? Didn't we have a Navy and an Army?

Once back at Frank's farm, he started to load the pickup with food and other essential supplies. Essential, if you intended to hole up somewhere.

"Where are we going, Frank?"

"Somewhere deep in the country. This place is too exposed."

"Have we been invaded?"

Frank turned deathly pale again, so he didn't have to answer. He didn't deny it, either. But I couldn't understand why he looked so frightened. Frank had fought in the last war like most of the men 'round here. He didn't talk about the fighting much, so whatever images crossed his mind when I spoke of invasion stayed inside his head. I trusted him enough to go with his judgement. If we were in danger—and Frank seemed convinced—then I wouldn't want to be anywhere else in the whole world. Though not because of his experience in the military, but because... well, Frank and I had an understanding. We hadn't acted on our natural impulse thus far, but we hoped that one day we would.

Frank slipped behind the wheel and started the pickup while I made myself comfortable in the passenger seat alongside him. We drove in silence for a while and then he turned on the radio, as if an idea had occurred to him. He found some band playing light dance music with a Spanish bent, the music pleasant enough but obviously not to Frank's taste, because he kept twisting the tuning dial. After a few minutes he became agitated, and I had to remind him to keep his eyes on the road. "Here, let me try. What were you trying to find?"

"Nothing in particular," Frank said, but I knew a lie when I heard one. I didn't pick him up on it. He reached over and turned the radio off. "I guess we're on our own," he said.

I didn't know what he meant, and I told him so. "I'll explain everything once we find someplace to hole up. You just keep looking out that window and let me know if you see anything suspicious."

"Like what?"

"I don't know. Flying saucers or them three-legged machines."

"Flying saucers? Now I know you're mad."

Frank just stared at me: a long serious stare to let me know he wasn't joking. I kept quiet for the rest of the journey, looking skywards mostly, looking for flying saucers of all things! A couple of hours later, we pulled off of the highway onto a dirt track that led to what appeared to be a disused barn. One of the large doors hung half off of its hinges, so we managed between us to pull the door open wide enough for Frank to drive the pickup inside. Then we reclosed the door. "What are we hiding from?"

"I told you, woman. Invaders from Mars!"

"No, you didn't," I yelled. Frank looked around as if making sure no one had heard me. For some unknown reason, I looked too. "Are you serious?" I said, keeping my voice almost to a whisper.

"I heard it on the radio. They've come in force, Martha."

"Isn't someone fighting them?"

"They tried. We threw the best we had at them and they wiped us out. Now we're at their mercy, though by the sound of the reports on the radio, they aren't showing us any."

"Oh, my God."

"Aye, praying may be all we have left."

"How soon before they get to us?"

"I expect there's still some pockets of resistance, so who knows?"

"Oh my. Jack!"

"He's probably gone," Frank said softly. "They took the cities first."

I dropped the cooking utilities I'd been unloading, stopped in my tracks with the sheer weight of the news. The death of my husband. The end of the human race! Frank came to my side. He put his hand gently on mine. "What's the point of this?" I asked him accusingly, as if the invasion had been his fault. "There's no hope."

"There's always hope." Franked smiled, one of those beaming smiles of his that always turned my knees to jelly. It suddenly occurred to me that Frank had come for me first. Despite the danger, he came for me! I rushed to him then, planting a big kiss on his lips.

"What's that for?" he asked.

"You know," I said. Then I did something preposterous. I told Frank I loved him. I had thought the words often, but I had never voiced them aloud. Frank smiled again. "I love you too, Martha." God, we are fated to die, I thought. If Frank openly admitted he loved me, it could only be because he thinks we have no future.

I finished unpacking the foodstuff. We ate a mediocre meal in silence. Neither of us had an appetite and, with nothing much left to say, we stuck to our own dark thoughts. We bedded down for the night. Frank had laid out some blankets on separate bails of hay, but I already knew we would sleep together, even if he didn't. He made to turn his back when I started to undress. "No," I said. "I want you to watch."

Frank turned around and sat on the end of a bail, watching me undress. He didn't say a word about why I wanted him to watch. I took my woollens, my dress, and petticoats off first. I then stood facing him in my underwear. Frank looked on in silence, but I caught him swallowing hard a few times. The loneliness must have been hard on him, remaining celibate since Maureen went.

For my part, I didn't feel as embarrassed as much as I thought I would. I had fantasized about lying naked with Frank, but I always thought the first time would be in some deceitful manner. This felt different because it wasn't premeditated. Even though I didn't know if Jack was dead or not, I couldn't miss this opportunity, for we would likely never get another chance. I removed my corset and my underwear and stood proud so my eager lover could see my nakedness. I lay on the blanket, inviting Frank over with a crooked finger. I watched as he undressed, having grown aroused with my own wanton display. Even after ten years of marriage, Jack and I had never made love with the lights on. I could clearly see Frank through the prevailing gloom inside the barn. I had to stifle a gasp as he removed his long johns and his cock stood rampant and erect. My own wetness grew, just thinking about what we intended. Frank joined me on the blanket, kneeling between my legs, his cock pointing at me like a large red poker. I reached for him as he fell next to me. I took his cock in my hand, stroking it gently. "Do you think God will forgive us?" I whispered. I asked the question for Frank's sake. I didn't give a damn if God forgave us or not. He seemed to have abandoned us anyway.

"We love each other," Frank said by way of vindication. We kissed then, his tongue searching inside my mouth for mine and then withdrawing after a short tussle. Feeling bold, I followed him with my own tongue, invading his mouth. We broke away for a moment. "Did Maureen ever use her mouth?" I asked, running my tongue along wet lips.

"She kissed real good."

"I mean on your cock."

Frank shook his head, said she hadn't. "Then allow me...." I slid down the blanket, kissing his chest on the way, sucking on his nipples until he cried out for me to stop. My own nipples ached something bad. I did my best to rub my breasts against him as I wormed further towards my target, kissing his abdomen, filling the recess of his belly button with drool. Then I reached his wondrous cock, bright red and angry looking, pumping with blood, with life. I took him into my mouth, feeling his heat, feeling the warmth of him dissipate as I went to work. I sucked on his cock the best I knew how. I had not sucked many cocks in my life, but I had put plenty of practice in on my husband. Frank arched his back, crying out when I raked my teeth along the length of his shaft, so I knew he enjoyed the wetness of my mouth. The ache between my legs grew in anticipation, sinful images running through my mind. With anticipation came wetness. I felt like a swamp between my legs. Hot and filthy wet. I reached out to touch myself, curling my middle finger into myself, drawing the hot honey onto my throbbing clitoris. I hovered there a moment, trying to imagine what it would feel like to have someone kiss me there—a recurring fantasy of mine.

I broke my reverie when I thought I heard a noise in the hayloft. Frank must have heard the noise too, for his eyes opened wide. We stayed frozen for a moment, then went back to our lovemaking when we heard nothing more. Frank grew tense each time I pushed him to the back of my throat, so I eased off, keeping him at a simmer, careful for him not to come in my mouth. I didn't mind if he did, but I needed far more from him. I eventually pulled away and crawled back up the blanket. Frank waited for me. I could tell from his eyes that the time had come. I rolled him over, pulling him onto me. I felt him hesitate a moment, then push forward into me, my wetness such that he slipped in easily. Then Frank went to work. After a few slow strokes, he grew a little frenzied in his desire to come. He pumped into me, gently at first, then when he realized I wouldn't break, with more conviction. I held onto his back, raking his flesh with my nails, claiming him as mine. Frank started to ram into me harder. I encouraged him by lifting my pelvis to meet each stroke. I knew Frank wouldn't last long, I could almost feel his body tensing for that explosive moment. So I slipped my hand between us, searching for my clit again, rubbing frantically, trying to catch up, but the sight and feel of me rubbing myself only forced the issue. Frank came with a tremendous burst of energy, pounding away like a man possessed. I felt his hot semen fill me and, still rubbing frantically on my clit, I followed him over the edge.

We lay entwined for several minutes, Frank between my legs, his cock slowly shrinking. I tried to hold onto him but he eventually slipped free, and I released my grip. We both sighed, drinking in the cool air, the perspiration tingling on our skin as the moisture evaporated. That's when I saw her. Hiding in the hayloft. I whispered to Frank and he made a lurch for the shotgun, waving it about in the general direction of the hayloft. "Come out," he shouted, "or I'll blow your fucking head off!"

His warning had the desired effect. A young woman crawled out from between the bails of hay. She descended the ladder gracefully and stood at the bottom, head tilted towards the floor. I had to laugh because Frank stood naked with the shotgun pointing straight out from his body. He looked ridiculous. I threw a blanket in his direction and he swiftly wrapped the material around him, not once taking his eyes off of the girl. "You can put the gun down, Frank. She doesn't look a danger to me."

Frank lowered the gun reluctantly, as if he wasn't certain of the girl. She definitely looked human to me, and a better specimen it would be difficult to find. She had beauty and figure. "What's your name?" I asked, pulling the other blanket over myself.

The girl looked up. Her face was redder than mine felt.

"Susan," she answered sheepishly.

"What were you doing up there?"

She didn't answer, but I could tell from her dishevelled clothing she had been doing something. "Were you watching us?"

Susan's face turned crimson, her eyes as wide as an owl's. "I'm sorry," she whispered.

"Have you heard the news, Susan?"

"Yes. I was so frightened I ran over here, and when I heard you arrive, I hid."

"So you've been here the whole time? You saw everything?"

Susan nodded, tears of embarrassment seeping from her eyes. Suddenly, she blurted out angrily as if she couldn't hold the words in: "I don't want to die a virgin!" She looked up then, keeping her eyes locked on mine, her face red with defiance.

I felt sorry for her, for all of our youth. "Don't cry," I said softly. "You don't have to."

She looked across at Frank and then back to me. "He's not much to look at," I joked, "but he has a cock, which I guess you've already seen, and he can be gentle."

"I'm scared."

"Of the men from Mars, or Frank?"

Susan smiled then. "A little of both, I suppose."

"Well, I can't do much about the aliens, but I can help you with Frank. I'll hold your hand if you like."

"He won't hurt me?"

"Not much. The pain is over so quickly, you won't really notice."

I glanced over at Frank. I could see his cock growing again at the thought of making love to this beautiful young woman. "Well," I said, "why don't you lie down here next to me and we'll get you comfortable." Susan remained hesitant. "We can stop whenever you want. Promise."

My promise seemed to appease her. She lay on the blanket next to me, remaining as stiff as a board. "Relax," I said, but just saying the word obviously wasn't going to work. Susan needed some help. "Have you ever kissed a girl?"

Susan blushed. "Once, at a fair, but that was only on the cheek."

"I bet you have a favorite boyfriend. In your dreams, perhaps?"

"Brad, Brad Thomas."

"Well, I'm going to kiss you now and you're going to pretend I'm Brad. Can you do that?"

Susan nodded her head.

I bent lower and started to kiss her gently, first on her cheeks, her eyes, her neck, her ears, working slowly towards her pursed lips. Susan gradually started to relax until my mouth met hers, and she tensed slightly. I kept my mouth there, teasing her lips with my tongue, enticing them apart until I could slip my tongue inside. She seemed to like the feel of my tongue so we kissed for quite some time, Susan gradually melting into my arms. I kept stroking her long hair, telling her what I intended to do, how she would feel when I did. I made up a little story, almost like a fairy tale. I enjoyed every moment. I hadn't intended to seduce Susan myself, but once I started kissing her, it seemed the logical thing to do. I looked up after a while. Frank had lain on his side watching us. I think his casual posture made Susan's seduction more exciting for me, having Frank watch me with a girl.

I gently, slowly slid my hand to her breast, squeezing the warm flesh lightly when she moaned into my mouth. I kept my mouth pressed hard against her lips to stifle any protest. Once she got used to my hand resting on her breasts, I squeezed harder, moving from one breast to the other, kneading them into pliable servants. Then when I felt certain I had conquered them, I started slowly to undo the buttons on the front of her dress. I think Susan had accepted her seduction by then, for she didn't attempt to stop me. In fact, when first I struggled, she reached to undo some of the buttons herself. She opened her eyes, smiling as I worked my hand beneath the layers of material to touch her flesh for the first time. Her nipple grew hard under my palm. I skimmed my hand over the protrusion for a long time, then when the nipple grew as hard as a button I squeezed the blood-engorged nubbin between thumb and forefinger. Susan opened her eyes with shock, but I had already changed back to soothing the inflamed flesh before moving on to the other breast.

With Susan's encouragement, I undid her dress completely. She wriggled free of the material, undoing the clasp of her bra, casting that aside also. Her beautiful breasts stood out proudly from her chest. She looked at Frank as if seeing him for the first time. Frank had pulled his blanket aside, fondling his cock openly as he watched Susan and me. Susan's eyes strayed to the beast between his legs. I just knew she wanted to touch it, but I wouldn't let her. Not yet. I pulled her back to me, cupping both breasts now, kneading them at will. My own ardour had risen again, so I pulled my blanket aside, offering my breasts to Susan. She didn't hesitate.

She reached for them, mimicking my own movements, pulling my nipples when I pulled hers, twisting them, silently challenging each other until we both became quite sore.

I broke the cycle by reaching between us to touch the top of her thigh, a mere finger's width from her sex. She opened her thighs for me willingly. I could see the moisture gathered on her underwear. I pulled at the material until Susan lifted her bottom and they came away. When I went back, I went straight for her pussy, running my fingers through her moisture, hovering on her clitoris as I like to do when I pleasure myself. Susan's excitement caused her body to shake. I slipped a finger inside her sex, then withdrew the digit, dipping into my own pussy, gushing now, before moving back to her pussy. I repeated the movements twice more before Susan caught on. Her hand slipped between my legs and she started to toy with me before pushing her finger deep inside.

We finger fucked each other for a little while, keeping the probing at a leisurely pace so Susan could relish in the newness of it all. All the time I thought about Susan pleasuring me with her tongue. I imagined her face between my legs licking where her fingers played. I took a risk. "I'd like to kiss you," I whispered into her mouth, "down here." I pushed two fingers into her sex to reinforce what I actually meant. Susan's eyes grew wide, but I saw the wickedness sparkling within the blue pools. I think that, overloaded with new pleasures, she had become willing to try anything. I got onto my knees, turned around so my face aligned with her pussy and hers mine. She looked so peach perfect, I didn't hesitate to dive in. I ran my tongue along the full length of her sex, trawling between her labia, gathering her honey onto my tongue. I swallowed the tiny pool I had collected, relishing in the taste of her.

I trawled deeper and deeper, each time edging my pussy closer to her face. She didn't have to lick me in return, I didn't intend to make her, but I truly hoped she would. I slowly worked my way to her clitoris, already inflamed and erect. I lashed out with my tongue and Susan made a little whimpering noise. I attacked the nubbin repeatedly, sometimes with long slow strokes, other times with little darts to keep her guessing. Susan's whimpering grew louder the longer I kept licking. Then I felt something touch my pussy and my heart began to race. I felt her tongue on me! She got straight down to business, finding my clit and sucking the throbbing flesh into her mouth. I almost came with her first touch, but I managed to hold back. I worked harder on her clit, trying desperately to make her come first. Nevertheless, Susan had a knack, or perhaps I just wanted to fall. She sucked on my nubbin, chewing the captured flesh between her teeth as she would a piece of gum. No way could I hold out. I came violently into her mouth, thrashing, trying to pull away from the sweet agony, but not willing to leave. In retaliation, I bit onto Susan's clit, a little harder than I intended, but the force of my bite coupled with my frantic wriggling brought her off. She exploded also, grinding her little cunt against my mouth for what seemed like an age.

We lay together a while longer before we heard Frank grumble about remaining left out. Susan and I untangled ourselves. She looked at me with those big blue eyes of hers as if she had discovered a goddess. I have to admit that I felt wonderful. Fed up of waiting, Frank made it perfectly obvious Susan had more to come. Susan lay back against me while Frank climbed between her legs. She held onto my hand as he positioned himself, squeezing my hand harder as he pushed forward. I could see the anxiety on her face, and then she let out a sudden gasp, her deflowering complete. I held on to her as Frank slowly built up a rhythm. "Careful now," I reminded him. Frank remained as gentle as I have seen any man. He slipped into Susan with measured strokes until her look of anxiety faded, replaced by a sense of wonder, I think.

"More," she whispered. I shot Frank a warning look, but still he built up speed. He had lost a little of his self control. I could hear his balls slapping against Susan's flesh. Susan opened her eyes. "There you go," I said, "you're fucking."

"I am, aren't I?" Susan raised her head to have a look at her pussy swallowing Frank's hardness. She watched Frank's cock slide in and out for a while, almost as if she didn't believe Franks cock could fit, before falling back onto the blanket. "Fuck me, Frank," she said. I could see that using those illicit words for the first time thrilled her. "Fuck me," she said again. Frank did, and, encouraged by Susan, he thrust harder and faster, until it became obvious that nothing I said or did would make any difference. I held onto Susan's hand as she wrapped her legs about Frank, letting him ride her full out. Frank didn't last long. I guess any man wouldn't with a beauty like Susan beneath him. Susan came too as Frank gushed into her, both of them crying out. It seems ridiculous I know, but I felt a kind of pride at the moment of their rejoicing. To think, I had participated in something beautiful, even as the world ended.

Later, we ate another mediocre meal. We talked about taking turns to stand guard during the night but decided against it. What good would it do anyway? Instead, we wrapped ourselves beneath the blankets and held each other tight. During the night, I felt movement. I realized that Frank and Susan were fucking again. I didn't feel jealous at all. I felt glad that two people at least had found some happiness. I pondered on how, when faced with hard times, we revert to the primitive. I prayed to God one last time to save us, hoping beyond anything else that people were making love all over the world. I thought it a lovely way to go.

Loud voices disturbed us the morning after. We all hurriedly got dressed. I grabbed Jack's shotgun and a box of cartridges, then waited with Susan in the darkness of the barn while Frank ventured outside to investigate. Quite some time passed with no sight of Frank or an invader. No shots fired. No dreaded heat ray. Nothing! After a time Susan and I heard voices, then howls of laughter. Frank appeared by the broken barn door. Susan and I waited with baited breath for him to say something. Frank, love him, looked more worried than he had the previous night. He walked over to our hiding place. "You can come out now. It was the Sheriff," he said. "They've been looking for us, Martha. You too, Susan."

"What news of the invasion?" I asked, wondering if perhaps

the tide had changed in our favor.

"Well," Frank said sheepishly, "you're not going to believe this. There was no Martian invasion. Apparently, it was some darn radio drama."

"So the world isn't ending?" Susan said gaily.

Frank looked at me. I looked at Frank. "I don't know, sweetheart. I don't know."

"I hear they let you go home after ten hours if you have kids, or even a pet to feed."

"Cinches it. Totally going to the pet store during my smoke break. You want me to pick up a hamster for you, dude?"

"Fuck no. You heard one of them things screech? Sound like my ex. What's the going rate on a bird?"

"Talking or not talking?"

Kyra listened to her two officemates chat, and her back curled lower and lower over her desk. Her index finger vibrated atop her ergo mouse. She tried not to think of how much she needed to ice down her wrists. Sleep kept pulling her eyelids downward, but she fought that bastard back. No way was she gonna let something as pussy as a need for sleep get in her way. This was her chance, her big opportunity: technical artist, not even contract, on a triple-A game title for a major studio. Her name up near the top of the credits. She had to nail this.

On the screen, she wrapped a new texture over the wire-frame model of this level's Big Bad. Pretty. Too pretty? Not edgy enough?

In her periphery, Zach knuckled his eyeballs. He hadn't shaved in weeks and looked yeti-like. She heard David yawn. Or groan, or something else she knew she didn't want to see. The guys were probably just as tired as she was, crunching for, what, seven weeks now? Fourteen-hour days, no weekends, bennie-prizes for people who stayed even later, longer, who put the pedal to the metal, put the 'we' in 'team,' and embodied other lame-sounding corporate speak, all with the goal of getting this game out the door.

Kyra tried to have sympathy for Zach and David and all the other guys working on *Bad Fairy*, but really, they were guys. They couldn't possibly get it. None of them had ever been the only chick in the uni computer science department. The only. None of them had ever deliberately cooled blushes when they rolled in one morning at god o'clock only to find that somebody had left a furry-muff porn screen saver up. On three monitors.

Nobody else in this whole damn building had to pretend that wasn't a turn-on. The guys, they just laughed it off, ribbed each other. Great fun, yeah.

Kyra's eyes glazed over, and she realized that her cursor had stopped moving. Weird. Her cursor never stopped moving, drawing, creating. It was a digital extension of her finger, of her imagination. It always did what she commanded. How could it be still? From a detached place at the very end of her string, she realized she was falling asleep. Sitting up. In her office chair. Zach and Dave were still talking, but they were no longer making words.

And then the office door leaned open, letting in a blade of fluorescent light from the hallway... and Lily.

Kyra woke up. Every fucking cell in Kyra woke up.

Lily was the Kevin-the-producer's assistant. She topped out at about five feet, had soft-looking, curly black hair and a killer little bod. But the really electric thing about her was her smile. She was always doin' it, too, grinning, even before the first pot of coffee, even after the last cleaning-crew vacuum sweep. Lily was always here, bubbly, keeping everybody's spirits up. Fetching things for Kevin, and for everybody, really. Kyra'd wondered more than once if she slept here.

Except that line of thought could get her in trouble because she'd start thinking about Lily in pajamas, then smaller pajamas, then slinky small pajamas... and her thoughts went down the gutter from there.

"How's it going?" Lily trilled, hauling all that light in from the hallway, but warming it up like natural sunshine. It crackled off Kyra's monitors, bleaching and flattening her game model. "Big Bubba's tonight, y'all. Tell me you don't *yearn* for BBQ."

"Just potato salad for me. Biggest vat of the stuff, please."

"Chopped beef, no pickles no onions no sauce no bread."

Leave it to Dave and Zach, respectively, to be totally unaffected by Lily's innuendo. Or maybe her words weren't really innuendo-laden. Maybe that was just Kyra's sleep-deprived brain supplying the breathy tone, the secret flirt. She liked how Lily had used the initials, not sounding out "barbie-que" and instead leaving some uncertainty there. BBQ... bright beveled quark? Big boobie queen? Bodacious buxom... oh, quit.

Lily leaned back against Kyra's desk and slid a menu onto it. Kyra tried not to notice the shallow impression the Formica edge pressed into Lily's skirt-covered ass.

"What can I get *you*, Ky?" See? There it was again, the breathy. The sexy. Only now Kyra could smell her, too. Not perfume, not even scented deodorant. Lily smelled like... lilies. Like walking in a garden right after the rain. That smell clanged so hard against the reality of Kyra's cave-like office that she almost got choked up. She wetted her lips and tried to scan the folded paper menu.

"Smoked turkey's good," Lily said. "That's what I'm having. And lots and lots of sauce."

Kyra felt her face get hot. Damn, she couldn't even summon the social acumen to order crappy crunch food. Was the job killing her, or had she always been this pathetic? She nodded and tried to say, "Yeah, sure, same for me," but it came out grunty.

She expected Lily, with her orders in hand, to rush off in her usual pixie scamper and start fetching things. Instead, Lily turned, faced the computer screen, and flattened her palms on Kyra's desk. LED light turned her face into a play of blues and deep pinks.

"She's hot, kind of in a domme way. I dig the leather flail." Lily was looking hard at the screen, but Kyra had clean forgotten what she was even working on. Or where she was. Lily's elbow brushed Kyra's shoulder, and sparks settled all over that side of her body.

"Yeah. Figured a fae wouldn't use a metal weapon, right?"

"Mmhmm. But..." Lily caught her bottom lip between her teeth for a second, and she turned to look straight at Kyra. Holy shit. Kyra couldn't even breathe. Her nipples peaked, and her toes scrunched up against the rubber of her flip-flops. "...you shouldn't make her wings red." Lily leaned in until her mouth was close, too close to Kyra's ear, and she whispered, "Fae wings only get red during orgasm. Blood flow and all that."

And then Lily was straightening up, retrieving the menus, reciting everybody's orders, and breezing back out into the hall. The door closed behind her, cocooning the game makers—two programmers, one tech artist—into their own dank little hell. Kyra almost convinced herself that she'd imagined that last part. Hallucinated it, really. After all, David and Zach were back to work like nothing even a little bit strange had happened.

But then she sucked in a breath, and the smell of flowers shoved her right back into that imaginary garden, and she knew that it had been real. Lily had literally, really, whispered into her ear.

Took Kyra about a minute to remember the contents of that whisper, and when she did, she decided she needed a smoke break. Right now. Didn't even matter that she didn't smoke.

Kyra was the only person on the fourth floor who used the ladies' bathroom. She knew this because once, just as an experiment, she'd held off telling anybody when the toilet paper ran out, and had just brought in little tissue packets for her own use. Three weeks went by before anybody thought to re-stock the ladies' room. She'd decided against performing a similar experiment that time when the overhead light went out. She wasn't hung up on her looks or anything, but every once in a while she needed to check her hair.

Lily must use the upstairs facilities. Made sense. Kevin's office was on five, right next to the super-secret executive board room. Lily probably had a desk up there, someplace.

At the sink, Kyra shoved her hands under a stream of cold water, got them good and wet, and then palmed her face. She felt hot, burning up, but buzzing like she'd just downed a half dozen Starbucks ventis. The faucet water didn't even begin to cool her down.

Her hands slid down, wrapping her throat, feeling the pulse push hard against her fingertips.

Thing was, even if she hadn't been deprived of sleep and real company—Zach and David didn't count—for almost two months, she still would have wanted to fuck Lily. This wasn't some cracked fantasy she'd thought up to dull the craziness of her work schedule. In fact, that first day last summer when Kevin had introduced her to his assistant, Kyra's mouth had flooded with wet, pooling up behind her teeth, and she'd wanted nothing more than to run her tongue all over Lily's body, to inhale and consume. It'd been all Kyra could manage to just half-smile and say hey.

And even then Lily's look had been knowing.

Could she? Could she really tell that Kyra lusted after her, and how hard? It wasn't the first thing on most women's minds when they met each other. Not that Kyra went around propositioning every succulent female who walked through her world—that would lead to heartbreak real fast—but she'd had enough romantic experience to be patient and make sure the other person was totally open to same-sex intimacy before she said anything remotely flirtatious. Most women, even those who'd been out a long time, approached relationships carefully. Kyra never wanted to offend.

But Lily had never let something like politeness hold her back. She'd been out of her bikini top before sundown at the company picnic. Granted, she was an equal-opportunity enticer, and could be bi, or even totally straight. After all, most guys were just as worked up about her as Kyra was. Only difference was that they could talk about it amongst themselves. They didn't feel a need to frig off in the bathroom, fantasizing about their co-worker. Or maybe they did. Kyra didn't really give a fuck.

Through drop-lidded eyes, she saw her reflection in the mirror. Her hair was coming out of its ponytail one strand at a time. It licked her forehead and neck, fringed her ears. Her face looked flushed, and she could see her nipples pushing hard through her bra and tee-shirt, just begging for someone to touch them. Kyra kept one hand around her throat, feeling the heat of her skin burn through her palm. The other hand crept south, over her tee-shirt, roving her bra, pinching one nipple, harder, and pulling it until she mewled.

She imagined Lily touching her like this.

She narrowed her eyes at her reflection, seeing herself as Lily would see her, and the background blurred. The dusky pink wall behind her closed in, embracing her, framing her. Fantasy gave that frame a shape: dark pink fairy wings, deepening to red.

Blood flow and all that, was it?

Kyra reached with both hands and grabbed her breasts, kneading, rolling her nipples until they burned. She needed more, needed other hands than hers, but this was all she had. She yanked her tee-shirt up and unbuttoned her jeans, flaying them over her sharp hip bones, exposing her trim, white panties. One hand dipped in. She saw the point of her knuckle and felt the fingernail graze her lips, her clit. She sucked in a breath and clutched the faux marble vanity with the other hand to keep herself upright.

Her middle finger slipped along the seam of wet, seeking the depths of her cunt, but the jeans still limited her access somewhat. Never mind, she could get off just rubbing her clit. And watching. And imagining that Lily was also watching. And touching. And coming, watching her. Kyra's hips tilted, driving into her fingers. She pressed her clit so hard that, were it another body part, she'd be leaving bruises for sure.

She climbed closer to release, so close, so hard that for a half-breath she didn't register the vibration against her thigh. And then, even when she realized that her phone was humming, her first thought was that, hey, that might feel good on her clit, shuddering her fairy wings to crimson. She just needed... Kyra let go of the vanity and pushed at the phone—still inside her jeans pocket—cramming it in toward her pussy, clamping her teeth as it grated over her hip bone. Fuckity-fuck: the pocket just wasn't wide enough. She yanked the phone out. Her fingers were already aiming it down her panties when she peeked at the illuminated screen.

A message from Kevin: *Kyra, 2 my office plz.*

Fuck.

❖

Kevin's door was open. It was always open. That was his policy. Sometimes the old farts tried too hard to be cool. Kyra rapped her knuckles on the door frame.

Some butterflies had set up shop in her belly, even though there was no way Kevin could know how she'd been spending her smoke break. If he knew, after all, that meant cameras in the bathroom, which was legally *not* cool. But Kevin wasn't the peeper type. Or was he? It hit Kyra all at once that maybe she wasn't the only person around here keeping secrets.

"Hey? You needed to see me?"

Kevin had his flip-flop-shod feet up on his desk and a tablet balanced on his thigh. When he looked up and saw Kyra in his doorway, he gestured for her to come in. "Have a seat, Ky. You already have dinner?"

"Um, no. Lily just now came around taking orders. I figure food's about half an hour off."

Kevin reached out with an unnaturally long arm and slid a dish along the desk. It was piled with cut fruit, and the waft hit Kyra's nose full force. Her mouth watered, and suddenly she was horribly, starkly, gut-churningly hungry. She sat down opposite Kevin and grabbed a mango wedge from the dish.

But eating one bite just made her hungrier. She shoved a second into her mouth, swiped the back of her hand across her lips, and forced herself to keep from reaching for more food. Despite some disturbing noises coming from her belly, she really didn't need to gorge right here in her boss's office.

"Better?" Kevin closed the tablet case and set it on a side table.

Kyra nodded.

"How's the level boss coming?"

Gotta change the wings. "Nearly done. I'll send you a composite before I leave tonight. I can put together some mock-ups for marketing tomorrow, if they need something."

Kevin's eyebrows may have twitched slightly, but hell, they were so thick Kyra couldn't be sure. "Lily told me you were having some palette issues."

Lily what? A surge of panic nearly had Kyra out of her chair before she settled herself. No, no, Lily probably said something about colors, but no way had she told Kevin exactly what she'd said. Kyra looked down at her hands, picked a loose thread on her tee-shirt hem. "Nothing I can't handle. I'm surprised she mentioned it."

Kevin took his sweet time replying, and Kyra didn't dare look up. Finally, he drawled, "She's interested in you getting this world right, Kyra. I am, too."

"Sorry," Kyra mumbled. How had this conversation become a treatise on her lack of vision? She was still on edge, jumped up from her bathroom break, and her defenses were down. Bitterness spiked. She had half a thought of telling Kevin off—of telling him that if he was so determined to stamp his own vision on this game, he could fucking well go down to her cramped, dark little office and knock himself out for fourteen hours a day, seven days a week. She didn't need his shit. She needed... to calm down. Damn, *damn,* where was her usual control?

She heard his chair squawk as he shifted. "Can I show you something?"

Kyra looked up before she could stop herself. Kevin was standing, holding out a hand. For some reason, she had this weird *Matrix* flash: red pill, blue pill, rabbit hole. Kevin looked weird, out of time and place, something magical.

And that's when my brain goes pop. "Sure."

Kyra followed her boss out of his very normal-looking office, down the hall to the next door, and then into a horribly normal-looking board room. Kind of cramped, though. Not what she'd expected from the super-secret executive meeting room, the holy of holies, where all the money guys got together to discuss the future of the studio's projects. Kevin didn't stop at the black-lacquer table. He went right to the overhead projector, reached below it, and fiddled with something there.

The projection screen hummed back into the wall, leaving a giant floor-to-ceiling gap. A secret passage on the fifth floor, downtown. Holy crap. Kyra blinked, but the doorway was still there.

"If you're very still, sometimes you can hear them from here, but the sound quality is loads better if you actually, you know, go inside."

He didn't need to push. Kyra could almost hear... music. Well, rhythm. She could feel it beneath the soles of her flip-flops. She could feel it in her bones. And there, pitched pretty high, a tinkle of laughter. Or a song? It was like ear-bleeding technojunk had mated with Disney to produce this gorgeous whorl of sound. Kyra wanted to hear it louder, wanted to dance inside it. Not even caring whether Kevin came in behind her, she stepped through the gap in the wall.

And everything she knew about the world and physics and reality exploded.

Fifth floor? Office building? Try Palladian whorehouse disco heaven. Blurs on the air that were kind of like clouds bore trays of fruit a lot like the one back on Kevin's desk. A fountain off to the right gurgled with blue stuff, and the closer Kyra got to it, the more it smelled like cotton candy. In every space, dancers writhed to the music, blurring bodies. She tried to concentrate on seeing just one dancer, but such focus proved impossible in this mosh.

A few of those bodies were clothed. Most mouths were full, of food or bubbles or blue liquor or someone else's body. Contortions of touch blew away everything a teen-aged Kyra had once learned from the Kama Sutra. Nothing, not even gravity, limited these people.

As her gaze panned the room, she came to the middle of the palace temple chamber, and her attention snagged on a dais. Vines of glowing blue stuff reached up from the misty floor, forming drapery around a platform that looked like it was made of pearl. Kyra blinked again, and the flashes of glitter on the air—things she'd assumed on first glance were bugs or confetti—resolved into tiny people with wings. Fairies. A least a dozen of them. Their wings were made of flickering light, all pulsing in rhythm with the music.

"This is the world we're trying to share with the mortals," said a voice from behind her left shoulder. Took Kyra a minute to connect that voice with Kevin. He sounded different here— different timbre. And then she realized that he didn't sound at all. Her ears were still full of the throbbing, piercing music, so full she couldn't possibly hear a plain, old human voice. Instead, Kevin seemed to be speaking directly into her mind. The sensation of voice was accompanied by a lick of heat along her spine. Sensory overload?

"Keep going. You're almost there."

Kyra did as instructed, rounding a pillar as she approached the pearl-topped dais and the edge of the vine canopy. And then she saw.

Slim foot, toenails varnished black. Round of calf, bent knee. And another leg, dangling over the far side of the platform. Kyra put her hand out and grasped the column for support, but she couldn't force her mouth shut as she looked her fill.

Lily, atop a mound of that blur-cloud stuff, her hair rioting over the pearl, her wrists bound by those slender blue vines. A fairy latched onto one breast, suckling it, whirring the air with the flutter of his—her? —wings. And as Kyra watched, another fairy flew in, attached itself to Lily's other nipple. Two more joined, nibbling, stroking with their tiny hands. For all the furious flutter, those wings also kept time with the music. Kyra wasn't even sure how it happened—she didn't know much about music, honestly—but hell, if gravity here was optional, maybe syncopation was, as well.

"She's fucking gorgeous," Kyra murmured.

"She's their queen."

The white of the pearl glimmered, mottled, and Kyra saw a flash of blue snake through it. On the dais, Lily opened her mouth and spread her legs wide open. Three fairies ducked into the lee between her thighs. Kyra tried for a better angle to see, but she could guess what they were doing. Her own clit thrummed in time. Clothes felt like bandages, bindings, shackles.

"It's okay. You can take them off."

Kyra forced herself to look away from the sumptuous display Lily was offering, but Kevin wasn't behind her anymore. She wasn't sure where he'd gone, but it didn't matter. She didn't feel abandoned. She didn't worry about getting back to the board room. Honestly, she didn't worry about anything. The music had invaded her blood, and the waft of cotton candy now carried an under-whiff of something dark and molten, patchouli and cannabis and... lilies. Well, of course, right? Dark lilies, though. Blossoming in sighs from the queen on the dais, rising as her chest rose with breath, unfurling from between her dew-damp thighs.

Kyra didn't remember taking her clothes off, but when she reached down to stroke her nipples, no tee-shirt got in the way. Thank God.

"Come up here. With me." The voice in her head wasn't Kevin anymore. It was Lily. "Come up here and show me what you're doing, Ky. Let me feast my eyes."

Kyra mounted the dais and found herself surrounded by fairies. They moved too fast for her to discern their sex, but things like gender identity seemed as bendable as physics here. No male/female, just bodies moving together, pleasuring and being pleasured in one mass of delight. Kyra had sworn off dick a long time back, but if one had slipped in from behind in that moment, she wouldn't have minded. Her whole body was electrified, ablaze and needing. In this place, she wasn't alone, the only girl, the only gay girl, the only anything. She was part of the greater whole. Part of the faerie queen.

A tiny fae tugged at her earlobe, shishing into her ear, tweaking a sweet spot of sensation just below, next to her head. Another found the pulse point in her neck and rubbed against it. Felt like the rough tongue of a cat, but warm and slick.

God, to feel something like that on her clit.

Laughter trilled in her mind. "Now you're getting it. We aren't bad fairies, we just like fucking. Open your eyes."

Kyra obeyed, and the fairies moved away, offering her a clear view of Lily's gorgeous pussy. Fat lips trembled with dew, and the hard bulb of her clit jutted through like a seedling, ripe and ready for tasting. "Suck it, Ky."

She didn't need prompting. Kyra climbed up onto the dais— what had seemed hard as pearl and gorgeously iridescent, gave under her hands, like skin. Warm, slick, pulsing with the thrum of the music and her own heartbeat, now, all one rhythm. Kyra spread her palms against it and breathed in the musky smell, mocha and lilies and cinnamon and cream. She nuzzled against the inside of Lily's knee, covering her face with the smell, with the heat. Her teeth raked across hot flesh, nipping, gnawing up inner thigh, roughing the tender, tender skin. The musk grew headier, thicker, hotter, as her face approached Lily's cunt, and the music's rhythm shortened, stabbed the air. Rocked her insides.

She felt fairies swarm her body, slipping against sensation points she didn't even know existed: the small of her back, the arches of her feet, her navel, her ears and breasts and hip bones and ass cheeks and calves and elbows and clit and pussy... God. She writhed against them but they were all over, everywhere, and there was no way to get leverage, to set the rhythm, to increase or decrease the pressure according to her will. She had no will.

Her mouth found succor and lapped, drinking in Lily's dew, suckling that delicious clit. Her chin dripped, slid along Lily's cleft. Beneath her palms, the dais pulsed. It warmed, hotter and hotter. She hollowed her cheeks, pulling hard on Lily's clit, digging her chin into the divot of her cunt, smearing her face, blurring their bodies like all the others in this room, in this world.

Orgasm erupted from at least a dozen epicenters, and Kyra's body and brain and universe shuddered hard, parting into a million pieces and reforming, glued by the strangeness of this place, the fury of emotion and sensation. Two things tethered her through it: the steady pulsing pearl skin beneath her hands and the tensed, shuddering body beneath her mouth.

"Come, my queen," Kyra thought, but her mouth was way too busy to make words. Still, she felt that Lily heard. Her hands melted into her wrists, bathed in fire. The heat was unbearable, but she heard Lily shouting, calling, singing, pounding out the rhythm of her delight.

Kyra tasted deeper, and Lily came.

"Lean back and look. See me."

Kyra opened her eyes. It physically hurt to pull her face away from Lily's still-throbbing cunt. She'd been caffeine-free a whole day before and hadn't jonesed for a taste like this. But Lily had asked, and Kyra wasn't about to say no. Not after this.

She rose up on her hands, looked down. The dais, which she'd first thought was white and then later decided was translucent with pangs of blue, now glowed deep crimson, a deeper red than she had ever seen, even on a light box. True red, blood red. Fuck red.

And this wasn't a weird skin-covering on a hard dais. It had shape. Wing shape. Beneath Lily lay her wings, burning vibrant red, filled with heat and orgasm.

Kyra stroked them reverently, helping her lover down from climax, settling into the slowing music, slushing sensory soup. She brushed a kiss against Lily's thigh. Lily laughed.

"Now then, art-girl, I think you can draw faerie."

"Damn right," said Kyra. "Just let me check that red again."

The nice thing about working the night manager shift at the Starlite Motel is that very little happens after hours. The bad part is that, well, very little happens after hours. I can kill time with paperwork and office cleanup—my daytime counterpart is a horrible slob—but after that? I get a lot of reading done. I know every late night radio show by heart, from Peregrine's Perch (classic rock hosted by a guy who's been stoned since Woodstock) to Phoebe Masters' Moonlit Classical Review. I've taken up and abandoned needlework, crosswords, Sudoku, and origami. My current obsession is solitaire, with a real deck of cards. In the long, quiet, dark hours of the night, you take such amusements as you can, always wondering what will happen to break up the monotony.

The Starlite Motel is located in a not-so-charming part of Puxhill, on Bishop Boulevard, just before it heads across the Grace River Bridge and into Covenant, which some call a suburb, some call a sister city, but all agree is a much worse place to be in general. We're about as far out and down as you can go and still be in Puxhill. We're cheap, discreet, and don't ask awkward questions. The folks that rent rooms (free local calls, A/C and heating, and HBO) tend to be desperate, on the run, on the skids, or out of options. Like me, once upon a time.

It was just past midnight on a breezy Tuesday in mid-September. I was looking for a home for the five of hearts, seriously considering a little innocent cheating, when the bell chimed to announce a visitor. I glanced up, expecting to see a guest looking for the ice machine, but the woman framed by the door was unfamiliar. Long experience allowed me to take her measure before she'd half-crossed the lobby. (You never know when you'll be describing someone for the cops.) Short and slender, she moved with nervous grace and underlying wariness. Dressed in worn sneakers, faded blue jeans, and what looked to be a black long-sleeved turtleneck under a red hoodie, only her head and hands were bare. Glossy black hair fell to frame pale skin and arguably Chinese features. She was young, barely an adult, and I recognized

The Runic Runaway
Michael M. Jones

the haunted, hunted look in her dark brown eyes: she was five steps ahead of trouble, one step away from disaster.

I swept the cards into a pile, putting them aside while giving the woman my most welcoming smile. "Evening," I said. "Welcome to the Starlite Motel. What can I do for you?"

"A room, please." Her voice was soft, without a trace of accent. Definitely a local girl.

I rattled off our rates. "Cash or plastic," I added, already knowing her choice.

Wincing, she dug into a pocket and produced a thin handful of cash. She counted it out in ones and fives, laying the last bill down with a sad sense of finality. There was nothing left to go back into her pockets. I gave her a sympathetic look, but nothing more; I'd been burned by fake sob stories in the past, enough to keep my guard up.

I took the money, exchanging it for a card. "Just need some basic information on here. Fill this out, initial the rate, sign it. Usual paperwork." I put the money in the register while she filled out the card. I knew it would be full of half-truths or outright lies; I'd have been surprised otherwise. You don't come to the Starlite Motel if you want to be yourself. When she slid it back to me, she'd left as much as possible blank, and listed herself as "Trixie Wheeler?" I looked up, eyebrow quirked, turning her name into a question.

Her skin flushed as she lowered her gaze to avoid mine. I was right. She was no Trixie. "I—"

I shook my head. "Hon, in the past few weeks, I've had three Michelle Obamas, a Martha Stewart, several Amy Winehouses, and I don't know how many Jane Smiths. It's nice to see someone with some creativity." I smiled warmly. "Nice to meet you, Trixie Wheeler. I'm Joanna Haven. If there's anything I can do for you while you're here, just let me know."

She lifted her eyes. The haunted look was briefly replaced by gratitude. "I'll be okay," she said. She took the key I offered, turning to head for the door and for the room I'd assigned her.

"Hey, Trixie." I surprised myself by calling after her. Every single time, I say I won't get involved. Every single time, I break that promise. She paused to look back. "You hungry? It's about time I took a break." I read the conflict in her expression. "It's on me."

That got me a quick nod. "Please. Thank you." At some point, she'd judged me and found me acceptable. That's usually how it is with me.

I took a moment to set up the forwarding system on our phones, so any incoming calls would go straight to my cell. It was a stab at modernizing the Starlite's ancient infrastructure; I'd pushed for the change when it became clear I'd be the only person responding at night, and couldn't always be in the office. I put up a sign further directing any visitors to call my number for assistance, locked up the money, and stood. "You might have noticed the diner on the other side of the motel," I said. "They're cheap, quick, and pretty tasty at this time of night. Theo, their cook, does a wicked Eggs Benedict."

"That sounds lovely." Trixie maintained her reserve, choosing her words as carefully as her movements, glancing around in anticipation of a surprise attack.

As I joined her, she blatantly studied me. My immediate thought was *I hope I pass muster*. I'm tall and curvy, with a little extra padding in all the right places. While my job doesn't lend itself to a lot of physical activity, I work hard to stay in shape. My Minnesota Swede father and African-American mother passed down an interesting blend of genetics; enough so that people have trouble pinging me on a first meeting. My hair's a tangle of brown curls, usually kept tied back out of sheer necessity and practicality. People say I have an understanding look, and comfortable features;

damned if I know what that's supposed to mean. It usually means "friend" rather than "object of desire," something I occasionally regret on the longer, lonelier nights. As usual when working, I was in jeans and a sweatshirt; the Starlite Motel's not one for a dress code and there's no one to impress. With Trixie's gaze on me, though, I felt the sudden urge to primp. Pride, perhaps. Or the stirrings of a much-neglected libido, which hadn't gotten the message that strays like Trixie were off-limits as far as I was concerned. It didn't help that she was a good ten years younger than me, either. With that sort of difference, I'm more likely to mother them than date them.

I shoved aside that train of thought, escorting Trixie to the Whistleberry Diner. She did a double take at the name, and I shrugged. "Back in the day, they specialized in bean dishes. Times and owners change, but the name lives on."

The Whistleberry is ancient as diners go, and has been around since the dawn of time, serving up hot food at cheap prices. It's no-frills, with everyone treated with the same mixture of casual disdain and neighborhood familiarity. The last time it closed, even for a day, was in 1987, for a family funeral. It was like my second home, after the Starlite.

Even at this time of night, there were a few other patrons. Most of them were at the counter, lost in coffee and newspapers and their own thoughts. We opted for a table. It took a few minutes, but we finally got some help. He was tall and skeletal thin, all in black save for the incongruous red and white apron they all wore here. With elaborate Celtic knot tattoos running up his bare arms, and enough facial piercings to set off an airport metal detector, he was the antithesis of the stereotypical diner waitress. "Tam," I greeted him.

"Jo." I wouldn't say he brightened to see me, but his posture went from deathly bored to vaguely alert. "New friend?" He jerked his head towards Trixie.

"Hope so. Start us off with coffee, while we decide?"

Tam took care of that. Trixie remained silent while he left, returned, left again, her hands folded neatly on the table. She kept her eyes lowered, more to avoid mine than out of any real modesty. When the menu came, she skimmed it for a long moment. Again, I saw indecision. I reminded her, "I'm buying. And I won't go broke on what they charge here."

That was that. Soon, she was digging into a massive combination breakfast. Eggs, bacon, toast, sausage, grits, all the good old standards. After singing its praises earlier, I naturally went for the Eggs Benedict. We ate in comfortable silence, Trixie devouring her meal like a locust. Eventually, she slowed down. Looking up from her ravaged plate, she met my neutral expression, and finally asked the question I was expecting. "What do you want?"

"Not a thing," I told her honestly. "It's nice to have someone new to talk to, now and again, but there's no debt between us. You're free to go at any time."

Trixie nodded. "Good." She ran a bit of toast through some egg yellow on her plate, nervously considering her options. Spill her secrets or keep them safe; we were now in the moment when things could go any which way.

"However," I said, "if you're in trouble, I might be able to help. If you're trying to get out of a bad situation, I know of shelters and safe places. I can point you at people who'll listen and understand. Or cops who'll take you seriously. Or I can loan you the money for a bus ticket." I dangled the information between us, let it sit while I stirred some sugar into my coffee. A minute went by. Two. I pointedly looked anywhere but at Trixie, while she continued her internal debate.

"It's not like that." She broke the silence with the thin, awkward admission. "I'm not sure who can help. Who to trust. How far I can—or should—run." Her eyes were wide, dark, and heartbreakingly lonely as they caught mine for a second.

"I have a lot of friends," I replied gently. "Some of them are used to really... exotic problems." This time, I made sure to capture her gaze, letting her read my expression and my intent. "You're free to walk away, Trixie. You have your room for the night, and in the morning you can move on. Do whatever you planned. If you had a plan." I paused, shrugging. "Or take a chance and let me do what I can."

"But why?"

"I'm a sucker for strays," I said honestly. "I try to make the world better, one person at a time. Someone comes to the Starlite, with the look you have in your eyes, I'd never forgive myself if I didn't at least give them a new set of options."

The pause this time was long, long enough for Tam to come by and refill our coffee, take away our dishes, and leave me the bill with a pointed look I ignored. He was really a nice kid, just a little rough around the edges. I'd helped him out of a bad spot, and now I was one of his favorite people, for what little it was worth. I'd tip him well for the time we spent here. Trixie fiddled with a straw wrapper, before making the next move. "I don't know why I'm running, or from whom. Three weeks ago, I woke up in an alley, hiding behind some trash cans, clutching a duffel bag full of my belongings. Every time I even think of going home, some instinct screams at me. Tells me to stay away. To run. To hide. To stay off the grid." Her knuckles turned white as her fists clenched; her eyes had that trapped animal look to them, and she glanced towards the street. "I've been on the move ever since. A night here, a night there. I had a wad of cash in my pocket, along with my credit and debit cards, cut up." Her smile was quick, bitter. "I'm not sure if I did it, or someone did it for me."

I gave her my full attention, projecting every ounce of sympathy I could. "You don't have any idea what happened?"

"Not a thing. I mean, I know who I am. I know that I graduated from Tuesday University last year. I know where I live, and where to find my family. But—" She slashed a hand in the air. "It's like someone tore out bits and pieces of my past. Even thinking about it gives me headaches. Even now, my instincts are going apeshit, telling me to get moving again."

My brow furrowed. "It sounds like some sort of post-traumatic disorder. Were you—?" I cut off the question as she shook her head.

"Untouched. Not a scratch, bruise, or sign of assault on me. I wish that comforted me. Because what I did discover was far weirder. The tattoos."

At my curious head-tilt, she sighed. She rolled up one sleeve, then the other, as far as the elbows. Unfamiliar runes danced along her skin, following curves and muscles organically. They came in a multitude of colors, almost alive in their richness. They continued under her sleeves.

"Sweet ink," said Tam, passing by to check on us. Trixie gasped, hiding the runic tattoos once again. "Whoa, sorry. Twitchy, much?" He sniffed, moving on.

"Impressive," I said. "Beautiful. What do they mean?"

Trixie's expression was bittersweet and forlorn. "I wish I knew. They... tingle. Often, I think they're whispering to me in a language I only know in my dreams. Sometimes they freeze, other times they almost burn. They glow in the dark, shimmer in the light, and when I'm not looking, they sometimes change shape or direction. No tattoo artist in town will take credit for them, and a few threw me out just for asking." She shrugged, as if shifting the weight of the world on her shoulders.

I didn't even know what to say. This was so far from my usual problems, I didn't even know where to start. My silence stretched on into the awkward range. Finally, "What else can you tell me?"

"Not a damned thing. Something within me wants me to flee, but something else is keeping me in Puxhill. I've been pinballing across the city for weeks, trying to dampen my flight instincts long enough to learn something—anything—and I'm out of money, out of energy, out of hope. I know without a shadow of a doubt that someone, or something, is coming for me, but not when or where or what or why." Her eyes shone with frustration. "So tell me how you can help me?" It was a plaintive demand. She expected rejection. I wondered if she'd extended her trust elsewhere, only to find laughter or disbelief. Sometimes, even once is too much. Or had paranoia's claws dug so deep into her that only I, with my "trust me" face and demeanor, could aid her? I placed my hand on hers, stilling its compulsive movements. I felt her relax under my touch.

"Trixie," I told her, "I don't know exactly what I can do, but I'm confident I can help." I released her hand, took up the bill. "Let's get back to the Starlite. We can plan better there." I paid, earning a nod of grudging thanks and see-you-next-time from Tam, and we left. Trixie leapt from her seat, as if glad to be on the move again.

Back at the Starlite, I checked on the office, just to make sure nothing had blown up, caught on fire, been vandalized, or otherwise gone haywire. All was as I'd left it. There were some nights when I didn't even need to be there. I escorted Trixie to my room.

I occupy a suite of two rooms, located next door to the office. Once they were units 1 and 2, but I'd been in them so long that they'd ceased to have separate identities, and were just mine. Neither was very large. Unit 1 served as a living room, where I entertained the rare visitor or stray, while 2 was my bedroom and personal space. I'd supplemented the usual crappy motel furniture with some secondhand pieces and local art, as well as assorted knick-knacks and personal possessions. With bright tapestries on the walls, an overflowing bookcase wedged into one corner, and other tokens of my existence, it was just like home.

I ushered Trixie in, shutting the door behind us and locking it. I shed my sweatshirt, tossing it over the back of a chair. Underneath, I was wearing a simple gray tank top. Comfy, but hardly fashionable, and it showed off a little more of my figure than I'd really planned. Screw it. I'd manage. Trixie was standing awkwardly in the middle of the room, so I waved a hand. "Make yourself comfortable."

Trixie perched on the very edge of the couch, wringing her hands. I went over to the bookcase, and ran my fingertips over the leather spines on the top row, where I kept my more esoteric finds. *Beneficent Charms. Wicked Beastes of the Night. The Gaslight District: An Oral*

History. *The Unspoken Mysteries.* They'd come to me one at a time, gifts from those I'd helped and serendipitous finds in used bookstores. When it came to magical things, I was a rank amateur, an untrained dabbler, but knowledge was power. I took down *Alderman's Rituals, Secrets, & Cunning Lore*, a thick book which threatened to fall apart in my hands, making a mental note to get it fixed someday. Gingerly, I flipped through it. First, to the index, then to a section near the middle, minding the pages ready to fly free. With a nod, I walked over to show it to Trixie. "What do you think?"

The pages I held open for her inspection were filled with a tight, barely legible script on one side, a passable sketch of a human figure on the other. The figure bore tattoos much like the ones I'd seen on Trixie's arms, though differing in the final design. Her eyes flew open, wide with recognition. She snatched the book from my hands, before giving me an apologetic look, her grip turning delicate. "This is them!" she exclaimed. She began to read, sliding a finger over the page as she puzzled out the faded words. "*Alio Lingua.* The Personal Language. According to this, we're all born with our own secret language. Unique words, syllables and phrases which define us intimately. We know it as infants, but it fades as we grow up and learn to communicate with the rest of the world. Maybe one in a million knows even a word of their personal language, most not even that." She paused, shivering, rubbing at an arm. "This sounds so familiar. I knew this. There was a spell. A way to decipher my *alio lingua*, to draw it forth from my soul and inscribe it on my skin. Blood and ink and... power." She looked back at the page, flipping it to read on. "To harness innate energy. To control, and exploit, and master someone and their potential."

She shuddered, and I rescued the book before she could drop it. "*Alderman's Rituals* is a damned spooky piece of work," I admitted, "but it's amazing what you can find in it. Someone stumbled across a copy years ago and actually put it online. Copies vanish almost as quickly as they appear, but once something's on the Internet, it's like a roach. I had a feeling that we'd find a beginning to our answers here."

Trixie nodded, fingers laced together tightly. "It's like a crack in the door," she murmured. "Someone... used me. But they didn't finish the job, did they?"

I skimmed the section, and shook my head. "The full process involves the face and hands as well. To 'claim dominion over the senses' and 'establish full mastery of the subject'. In other words, if they complete the ritual, you're little more than a meat puppet, dancing under their command. Gods, what a mess."

"Just enough to keep me from running far away. I struggled. I fought. I fled. And somehow, in the process, I tore open my memory like a newly stitched wound. Thoughts bleeding all over the sidewalk. My enemy's identity lost."

"There's more," I said. "Not much, but...." She nodded. I went on. "The subject may still be controlled through intimate contact, to stir the mind, inflame the senses, and raise the power."

Trixie's expression shifted from sour to thoughtful, as something sparked in her eyes. "There was a woman," she whispered. "Fingers sweeping over me. An electric touch. Her mouth on my skin. Where she kissed me, I blazed to life. My blood boiled with desire. I loved her. And she did this to me."

My own muscles tensed as Trixie's words conjured up dangerously tempting images. My long-ignored libido shifted, stirred like a snake on a sun-warmed rock. I forced myself to breathe easy, to ignore the thought of Trixie caught up in passion, in the throes of orgasm. I closed the book with a little more force than was necessary. We both jumped a little at the sound, and the mood was broken. Nervously, we glanced around, then back at one another.

"I have a thought," I said. It was a bad idea. Scratch that—a horrible idea. And yet, what alternatives were there?

"To stir the mind, inflame the senses, and raise the power?" asked Trixie, as if reading my thoughts. Her lips twitched in a soft, wry, bitter smile before her expression hardened; she was pulling away from me again.

"Hold on," I said, hands up in reassuring protest. "I promise you, I don't want your magic. I don't want to use you. Honestly, it's about the last thing I want. I don't need anything more than I have here and now. I swear." I gave her a moment to think about it. "I'm just exploring our options. I know people who could fight for you, who could find your mystery woman and turn her into chopped chutney just for blinking funny. They could send her packing, or they could leave her a drooling vegetable. Problem is, it takes time to get in touch with some of them, while calling on others would incur a debt neither of us is eager to pay. I can do it, though. Say the word, and this can all go away. I'm sure one of them could also restore your memory."

"Or I can trust you, and we can do this together?" asked Trixie. She sounded hopeful, leaning forward to give me a look mostly free of suspicion.

"I've dealt with my fair share of things that go bump in the night. If we work as a team...." I didn't explain any further. I had certain rules, rules that kept me sane and relatively content at the end of the night. I only helped those willing to accept it. I didn't solve all their problems for them; I gave them whatever tools they needed to make the next step. A phone number, a bus ticket, a safe place for the night, an introduction. That sort of thing. I knew that the best kind of success was the sort you were willing to achieve on your own. If Trixie really wanted her freedom, she'd need to do it herself, not have someone else come in guns blazing. I gave her the choice, and....

"You're right. It makes sense." Trixie shrugged out of her hoodie, dropping it to the ground. She grabbed the hem of her turtleneck, and paused. "I haven't let anyone else see me like this. That I know of. I—"

"Want me to look away?" I offered.

That provoked a laugh from her. "You'll be seeing it all soon enough. Um. Talk to me? Distract me? Why do you do this? Helping people? Living in a shithole motel while giving aid and comfort to people like me?"

I couldn't even take umbrage at her dismissal of the Starlite; it really was a shithole, unapologetically so. I leaned back against my chair, keeping my gaze neutral while I found my beginning. "It all goes back to high school. I was much younger and stupider. I slept with the guy I loved, and was seven months pregnant when I graduated. We got married, and thought we'd do okay."

Trixie pulled the turtleneck over her head, displaying the plain white bra underneath. The runes covered her from wrists to neck, tracing curves and vanishing under the fabric of the bra. There was an alien, exotic manner in how they outlined her body, how they drew out her very essence. On her own, she was attractive—slim, well toned, with smooth pale skin, and small breasts—but in a girl-next-door sort of way. The tattoos transformed her and set her apart. She saw the look in my eyes, and froze, self-conscious. I quickly continued.

"When Alexandria was five, I fell in love with another woman for the first time. That's a long story in its own right. It took me a while to work through everything, to tell myself the truth, that I was bisexual, but really preferred girls. Samuel—my husband— took it badly when I tried to talk to him about it. I... refused to change just to keep him. I refused to deny who I was. He demanded a divorce, and got one. His family, who'd never liked me, was able to afford a much better lawyer. He got everything. Including my baby girl." The memories still hurt, as raw as though they'd happened yesterday.

As I let my sob story unfold, Trixie shucked her shoes and slithered out of her pants, revealing the panties to match the bra. Much-worn, often-washed, clearly at the end of their lifespan. The runes wrapped around her hips and legs, ran down thighs and calves, and ended at the ankles. I took a deep breath, trying to ignore the stirrings of desire deep within. "I could have fought them. Even then, it's not like being a lesbian was enough to lose custody, except Samuel's family had the judge in their pocket as well. I was in a pretty bad place, and spiraling downward in a hurry. I let them win, and fell apart. Eventually, with nowhere else to go, I ended up here, exchanging cleaning work for a room. Then the night manager spot opened up, and I pressed for it. Got it, to my surprise. Been here ever since. I've made a new life for myself. It's not perfect, but I'm happy. And when someone crosses my path, hurting and alone and needing that single bright moment in the darkness of their life, I try to give it to them."

Trixie unhooked her bra and let it fall from her arms, exposing her tattooed breasts. Her nipples were dark and erect, standing out against the runes which entirely circled them. She stepped out of her underwear, and I noticed she was shaved bare, with runes reaching between her legs as if drawing power from her female center. For a brief, giddy second, I saw her as the outline of a woman, rendered all in silver lines, lacking just the head and extremities to be whole. I blinked, and she was back to normal again. Exposed, vulnerable yet strong, she held herself still like a classic statue. Her dark eyes bored into mine, lips half-open as though words balanced on the edge. What she said then surprised me. "You know what, Joanna? You sound lonely."

"I what?"

Trixie took several steps in my direction, delicate and purposeful. "Here I am, scared shitless, worried for my sanity and my freedom, running for my life, and you're a candle in the dark. And yet you sound so lonely inside. Mothering other people. Helping strays. Taking on their problems. It's like you're trying to fill the void left by the loss of your family, but in a way that doesn't require actual commitment."

"I what?" I repeated, brain stuck in neutral. I wasn't sure what I'd expected from Trixie, but a cutting analysis wasn't it.

"I learned a few things in college," she said, lips half-quirked in a faint smile. "I remember that part." She came to rest in front of me. Taking my hands she tugged me to my feet. "I believe you don't want to use me. I see how you look at me, attracted, but hiding it. Refusing to think of me as a way to gain power. But you were right. We don't have time for propriety or delicate sensibilities. We can't hold back." She placed my right hand on her hip, my left over her heart. The runes underneath shone, electric-warm to the touch, my fingers tingling. As the power stirred to life, she tilted her head up, whispering, "Please enjoy this, Joanna. I'm giving myself to you." Her eyes were filled with a longing; she wanted the moment as much as I suddenly did.

Our lips met in a slow, soft kiss, and her body melded to mine, her slight frame nestled against my generous curves. Instinct took over, my fingers sliding over bare skin, following the lines and twists of the runes. Silver light gleamed as each in turn activated. Runes blazed along her sides, her waist, her rear, and the full length of her spine, following the path of my hands. Her lips parted to invite a deeper kiss, and I accepted gladly, tongue teasing hers in a playful dance. I breathed in a scent uniquely hers, one escaping words, and my head swam. She laced her arms around my waist, holding me to her, as if I'd be going anywhere at this point.

Breathless, we broke apart after several long minutes of kissing and touching. "For this to work," she gasped, cheeks flushed and eyes bright, "you should be naked also. The more skin-to-skin contact, the better."

There was logic I couldn't argue with. She tucked her hands under my tank top, drawing it up and over my breasts, tugging it off altogether. Her touch was invigorating, my nerves blazing in her wake. It had been a long time since a woman—since anyone— touched me like this; I almost didn't notice when she unclasped my bra and encouraged me out of it. My breasts spilled free, lush and heavy, aching with long-denied need, and she soothed them with gentle touches and light kisses. The moans escaping my lips brought a true smile from her; that was enough to spark me to life. Together, we shed the rest of my clothes, letting them fall where they might. Together, we stumbled through the connecting door and into my so-called bedroom. I barely had time to be grateful I'd cleaned up recently, before we fell onto the bed with a crash of springs and laughter.

Once neither of us was holding back, the sparks flew. Literally: as I explored Trixie's body with hands and mouth, the runes gleamed brighter and hotter, their energy streaming into me with every point of contact. I was charged, electrified, empowered, overflowing. She encouraged me with moans and whimpers, pushing herself against me, fingers raking along my sides. I realized just how much of her guarded demeanor had been an act, her passion burning it all away. How could I not respond to that? How could I not give as good as I got? As her legs parted, I followed the runes with my fingertips, seeking the source of her arousal, of her warmth. A low cry of approval slipped from her lips, her hips arching upwards in blatant offering. I stroked her, finding her slick and hot and ready. When my fingers entered her, she gasped, tensing around them, trying to hold me tight. We rocked together as I alternately fingered her and rubbed her clit, coaxing her into a very real, very powerful orgasm. The power exploded out of her, soaked up by my body, rushing out of her sex and up through my fingers, into my core.

The sheer pressure of the magic as it found its home in me was enough to disorient me; in that moment, Trixie seized the opportunity to get the upper hand. Before I knew it, her lips were blazing a trail over my breasts, tongue flicking over super-sensitive nipples, leaving them taut and aching as she moved onwards. Slender fingers moved with experience and purpose over my skin, stroking and caressing. I stretched out on the bed, understanding that this was as much for her as for me, a way of recapturing something she'd lost before she ever met me. My nerves tingled, my body blazed, and every touch left me wet and wanting more. She rubbed herself against me, breasts brushing against mine, leaving me all but helpless under her attentions. By the time she buried her face between my legs, I was lost in a sea of sensation. Her tongue teased, tormented, tasted me with long strokes and quick flickers, keeping me on the edge for long moments. Then she shoved me over the edge into an earth-shattering, mind-searing orgasm, annihilating and remaking me in the space of a second. When I returned to my senses, I was sweat-soaked, shivering, and saturated with magical power.

Moreover, I had knowledge that hadn't been there before. I

looked at Trixie, and I knew her. I saw her soul and the collection of choices that had made her; it about made me weep for the strange beauty that was humanity. I knew how to cast curses and charms, spells and hexes. I instinctively understood how to change reality with the crook of a finger and the utterance of a syllable.

It terrified me.

I wasn't meant for such things. I didn't trust myself with the power and the responsibility. I wanted to give it back. Immediately.

Then I met Trixie's eyes. I saw the hope and trust she'd placed in me. She hadn't opened herself up to me, she'd given me everything. I'd become her champion.

More importantly, she knew herself. I saw things flickering behind her eyes and in her mind. A cascade of memories, a kaleidoscope of images, a multitude of realizations.

I kissed her. Slow and soft, holding myself to her lips, and then forehead to forehead. Trixie spoke, her words trickling forth. Hesitant at first, but then with more confidence. "Eleanor. She was my roommate all throughout college. And my lover. I was... young and foolish and on my own for the first time, and she was dynamic and exciting and everything I'd ever thought I wanted."

I felt Trixie's rush of freedom, her intense joy at understanding who she was and what she wanted. I felt the intoxication of love, and the whirlpool of desire, and I knew exactly how Trixie had drowned in it.

"She introduced me to all sorts of things. Including magic. And I went along with everything she suggested, because I loved her, and didn't think any better of it." Trixie looked past me, seeing everything she'd forgotten. "I came out to my family when I was a junior. They... didn't take it well. I didn't have any other real friends, Eleanor saw to that. Gods, she spent four years isolating me, conditioning me, turning me into a tool." She shuddered against me, and I held her close while she composed herself again. I saw the shadow of Eleanor looming large over Trixie, and I understand what manner of person she was. Her sort always excelled at doing nasty things to others.

"I knew something was wrong near the end. I found out what she had planned. I ran, but fighting her control took its toll on my memory in the process. I've been running ever since." She bolted upright, eyes wide. "She's coming. I can feel her plucking at my strings. Something wicked this way comes."

Instinctively, I understood that Eleanor had come in response to our ritual, feeling Trixie's power through their arcane connection. My solution had hastened the confrontation. But this was my territory; we held the advantage. I hoped.

We climbed out of bed, dressing in hasty silence. "Let's go tell your ex it's over," I said. Trixie flashed me a quick, thankful smile. I squeezed her hand for comfort, before we exited into the parking lot.

Eleanor was almost disappointing in her lack of menace. She was of average height, a stocky short-haired brunette with pale skin and icy blue eyes. She was wearing black leather pants and high-heeled black boots, a black corset that showed off way too much cleavage, an abundance of silver jewelry, and bright red lipstick. It was all way overdone. She had a remote attractiveness to her, but I knew her type well. Always trying to be queen bee, always failing. Never quite making cheerleader. Never the prettiest. Always reaching for the stars, and never escaping the gutters of her mediocrity. The sort to blame others, to use others, to steal power, to always take, never give. There was a cold intensity to her, an aura of power that magnified her natural presence.

She looked from me to Trixie, back again. "I don't know what she's told you, but stay out of this," she demanded. "It's not your business. Merely a... lover's quarrel." To Trixie, she said, "It's time to come home."

Through the bond Trixie and I now shared I felt Eleanor tugging at those strings, trying to influence her. They strummed with conditioned power. Trixie stiffened, her eyes pleading with me even as she tensed to take a step. I saw the wicked way in which Eleanor had ensnared her, a delicate tangle of emotional and psychological ties bolstered with magic. I saw how she teased the strands, imposing her will.

"I'm afraid it's not as easy as that," I told Eleanor. "Trixie's rejected you and your hold over her."

"Trixie?" Eleanor's laugh was an amused bark, derisive and contemptuous. "So you don't know who she really is? Who her father is? Why she's such a perfect little helper? Don't you know *anything*?"

I could, if I wanted. Trixie's soul lay bare to me. It would be the simplest of things to rummage through her mind and memories. To betray her trust, to disrespect her privacy. I'd already seen and learned so much, but only what Trixie wanted to share. "Can't say it's pertinent, under the circumstances," I said with a shrug. "She says her name is Trixie. And she very definitely wants nothing more to do with you." A slow smile blooming on my lips, I used Trixie's power, reaching out and severing Eleanor's hold. The strings connecting them snapped, one by one. Trixie's gasp was one of relief; Eleanor's cry was one of disbelief. She jerked with backlash. The tension between them vanished in a second. "Frankly, I don't think much of your hobbies," I continued.

"You—You *bitch*!" Eleanor spat out. She gathered up her own stored power and focused it. I felt the waves of anger sweeping towards me, a spear of pure hate speeding towards my heart. "You goddamned fucking nig—"

I brought both hands up swiftly, blocking the attack with a shield created from borrowed magic. Promptly lashing out, silencing Eleanor with a compulsion of my own. "If you can't say anything nice..." I threatened. "Be glad I didn't let you finish whatever hateful shit was about to really piss me off."

Eleanor turned her baleful gaze on the two of us, magic crackling feverishly on the air as she readied another strike. I took Trixie's hand; the next attack flowed through us, dissipating harmlessly as I grounded it. Together, it was child's play for us to follow the trail back to its source, drawing out the rest of Eleanor's power, draining her. Just for good measure, I wrapped Eleanor in several layers of geasa and compulsion, preventing her from ever touching the magic again, barring her from exploiting anyone else.

Empty, helpless, crying tears of silent fury, she stumbled backwards, falling to the ground in a heap. I released Trixie's hand, crouching before Eleanor. "You can be a better person, you know. This is unworthy of you. Now that you can't steal anyone else's power, you'll have to find some way of standing on your own, and doing things honestly. I can help."

She glared balefully and reared back, lips pursed as if to spit in my face. I sealed them with a simple tap of the finger to her mouth, and she spluttered instead. "Then again, maybe you need a cooling off period first." I sighed, standing again. I wove one last spell around Eleanor, a compulsion to go home and remain there for twenty-four hours. I unsealed her lips, but warned her, "The silence will last until you get home. Consider it my way of making sure you behave yourself." I glanced over. "Trixie? Do you have anything to say to Eleanor before we send her on her way?"

Trixie stalked over to deliver a rousing slap, leaving Eleanor's cheek stinging and red. "We are so through!" She gave me an amused look. "Anything more would be unworthy of me, like you say. She's defanged. Get rid of her."

Just a little sorry that it had come to all this, I activated the spells I'd set on Eleanor. Red handprint still blazing on her cheek, she stiffly turned, marching over to her car, a battered blue Volvo with the license plate "WITCHY." *Subtle*, I thought. She'd probably want to change that. She peeled out at top speed, leaving Trixie and me behind.

"Now what?" Trixie asked. In the east, the sun was starting to poke over the horizon.

"I go back and pretend I was actually in the office all night, until the day manager gets in. Then I get some sleep. You should sleep also. It's been a hell of a long night for all of us."

Trixie looked at me thoughtfully. "And that's it?"

I nodded. "That's it. Tell me how to give back your power, and it's all yours, every last drop." I watched her relax, and smiled. "Like I told you. Don't need it, don't want it."

So that's how things played out. She took my hands, and I poured every ounce of magic back into her, the energy and knowledge rushing out of me like a drained water tank. As we did so, I made a little tweak to things, showing her how to control and wield her own magic, so she'd never be at the mercy of outsiders again. The process left me near-exhausted, and it was a real effort keeping awake until the next shift came on duty. Trixie was already asleep in my bed by the time I joined her; I curled around her, and slept like the dead for the next few hours.

When I awoke, the bed was empty, and had been for a while. There was a note waiting for me on the dresser.

Joanna—I'm leaving Puxhill for a while. Now that I'm free of Eleanor, it's time to rebuild my life. No offense, but I'd rather be far from you as well until I figure it out. I need to do this on my own. Don't be upset, I took just enough money for a bus ticket like you offered. I'll pay it back when I'm able. Wish me luck. And please, take care of yourself. Don't be so lonely.

 -Trixie

I don't know where she went, or what happened to her next. I don't know her real name, and I've never tried to figure it out, despite the hints. To me, she'll always be Trixie. I hope she's happy, and in control of her life.

I've seen Eleanor a few times since. She comes to the property line of the Starlite Motel, and stares at the office. There's a longing in her expression that I know well. But she always turns and walks away again. One day, she'll make up her mind. Will she come seeking help, or revenge? That's anyone's guess. Guess I'll find out on the day she comes in with an open hand, or a loaded gun.

Either way, it'll be an interesting night.

There she was, archvillainess Samhain Kiss, right in front of me on the dance floor at Sappho's. Grinding her hips in a way that was undeniably sexual, even though she was dancing by herself.

Ah, the irony. I was dressed as Healing Fire, superheroine and Samhain Kiss's arch-nemesis.

That gave me the perfect opening line. I summoned all my alter ego's courage and crossed the dance floor to my sexy costumed stranger.

She was facing away from me when I got there, so I tapped her on her bare shoulder. When she turned, long black-and-electric-blue hair whipping dramatically, I said loudly, "Samhain Kiss, you're under arrest for being too hot for your own good."

She stopped moving, looked me up and down in a way that made me shiver with pleasant anticipation. "Oh," she said, making a face of mock-alarm, eyebrows high and mouth forming a pouty, kissable O. "The horror! Whatever will I do?"

I put my hands on my PVC-clad hips and widened into a superheroine stance, legs apart. "The penalty is...dancing with me."

"You've won this round, Healing Fire," she said, tossing her hair again and crossing her arms under her leather bustier so her breasts plumped up beautifully. "But I'll find a way to thwart you, just you wait."

Some might have guessed it was luck that right then the DJ put on a slow song. I knew better. I knew it was wrong, but I used my power of telepathy for personal gain, just this once.
Because I *am* Healing Fire.

It's all the outfit's fault. The short, shiny white PVC "nurse's uniform" with red flames—it looked like something you'd find in a high-end fetish boutique—was magic.

I don't understand exactly how it works. All I know is that the uniform finds you, appears in your closet like it had in mine six months ago, and makes you more than you ever dreamed of being.

It gives you firestrikes and secret martial-arts techniques to fight archvillains, healing powers to protect you and save crime victims. It makes you a superheroine, in short. And when you're

Pow! Bash! Yes, Yes!
Sophie Mouette

ready to retire from Superherodom, you wake up one day and the uniform is gone, moved on to the next Healing Fire.

So why was I wearing it at the Halloween party at Sappho's? I'd just come off a long shift helping Ceridwen and Technomage fight some of Samhain Kiss's minions, who'd been trying to do something complicated and evil involving nanotechnology and the spirits of the dead. I was fried, I really wanted a beer, and I'd forgotten to bring regular clothes with me when I'd gone flying out the door to the crime scene. So I put my Distraction Glasses on, and went to my favorite bar as Maya-Simkin-in-a-costume.

The Distraction Glasses came with the outfit. Some secret technology made you look subtly different when you put them on, so no one connected you with your alter ego, even though your mundane and super faces were identical. That explains Clark Kent and Superman, right? Pre–Healing Fire I'd worn glasses, so no one would think anything of it.

Samhain Kiss's outfit was pretty damn good, too: all black leather and silver lace and fishnets and boots. I'd never met the real Samhain Kiss, and she'd never been photographed because one of her powers fried cameras, but this lady had done an awesome job creating a costume that looked like the police composite sketches.

Only under the stark white makeup and the lipstick so dark red it was almost black, she was a lot prettier than the police sketches. Her curves, shown off by the leather bustier and long, artfully tattered lace skirt, were more impressive than any of the eyewitnesses had reported.

Then again, would you notice her figure while you were fleeing her flesh-eating technozombies?

Enough of that. This was far, far better than the beer I'd planned to use to wind down. Especially when, in reaction to the slow song, she put her arms around my waist and snuggled up against me.

Curves against curves. Leather against PVC. Skin against skin. We moved together through the slow song, just dancing at first, but gradually slipping into a more grinding-together sort of movement. And when the music changed and the other slow-dancing couples moved apart, we didn't.

Let me tell you, it takes determination to slow dance to German techno.

Determination or small, strong, skillful hands gripping my ass through PVC while I stroked hers through lace. Her leg slid between mine, teasing against my PVC-clad pussy. Yes, the outfit came with matching flame-patterned undies. The Superheroes' Union told me they were very important, even if cotton seemed more practical. For the first time ever I was glad I'd listened. The PVC made me extra aware of how wet I was getting, and made the teasing seem kinkier.

The combined smells of leather, PVC, and two sweaty, aroused females rose between us. She was wearing some exotic perfume, like Stargazer lilies and myrrh and spices, and it went right to my clit.

I'm not sure how many songs crashed over us as we stayed like that, swaying and clutching and reveling in each other's nearness. I know we only stopped when the DJ cut the music to announce something.

We stopped and looked into each other's eyes.

Hers were dark, dark as the grave, pupil-less with a hint of red.

I almost pulled away, but remembered that I'd seen ads all over for special Halloween contacts. Devil eyes, kitty-cat eyes, superhero or villain eyes—you name the look. For a small fee and a visit to your eye doctor, it could be yours.

"You have such pretty eyes," my raven-haired beauty whispered. "Would you take off your glasses so I can see them better?"

Take off the Distraction Glasses? So not a good idea! "I'm blind as a bat," I lied. "Makes me nervous."

"I'll take good care of you," she promised.

Then she raised her little hand, with its short black Gothy nails, and slipped them off me. "They're not pretty," she breathed. "They're beautiful."

And before I could protest, she covered my mouth with a kiss.

She tasted of cheap lipstick and Chardonnay and something else, something I couldn't place.

I forgot all about my glasses and clung to her, as her kiss lit a fire in my belly.

I was dizzy from arousal and the power of her kiss.

Literally dizzy.

The room began to swirl and spiral, and the air jangled in a way that meant I was about to be teleported.

Oh shit. She wasn't wearing a costume, either.

Then I blacked out in the arms of Samhain Kiss.

Damn her kiss!

I woke in Samhain Kiss's lair. So far, nobody had been able to find it. Given the position I was in, I couldn't tell you where it was, just what it was—an abandoned Gothic cathedral. Gotta admit it, that was some serious flair.

Fat white guttering candles in various ornate holders surrounded me like I'd been trapped in an old Police video. From somewhere far, far above, in the rafters that were probably too shadowed to see even in daylight, I heard the rustle and coo of pigeons.

And then there was Samhain Kiss. She was standing at an old lectern, the kind with a gold eagle with spread wings at the front, staring down at me.

As for me, I was bound spread-eagled to a wrought-iron bedstead. The deep red brocade coverings smelled of vetiver and dragon's blood. Curiously, I was still in my PVC superheroine outfit. Wasn't that typical of an archivillainess, though? So confident of her own powers that she hadn't bothered to strip me of the things that gave me my powers.

When she saw that I was awake, she turned and walked down the spiral stone steps.

My mouth went dry when I saw she was tapping a riding crop against her boot.

Perhaps she'd been waiting to strip me until I was conscious. Despite myself, I shivered. All the way down between my legs. Swollen and slick, my cunt lips pressed against my PVC panties.

"Pretty, pretty Healing Fire," she murmured close to my ear, running the tip of the riding crop along the deep vee of my cleavage where my outfit pressed my breasts together. Really, whoever had designed the costume had no idea how difficult martial arts could be with your boobs on a platter. Which meant the designer was a man.

The crop teased that sensitive flesh, sending little jolts of panicky pleasure careening around my body.

My brain was clear: Samhain Kiss, gorgeous and seductive as she was, was an enemy. My nerves endings, unable to get past the concept of *really hot woman who wants some kinky fun*, vibrated with delight.

"I've been watching you," she went on, tip-tapping the flippy end of the riding crop lightly across my quivering stomach. "You were very, very naughty today, taking out my henchmen. It was just pure luck that you came wandering into Sappho's tonight. I've been wanting to punish you."

She sounded like the script for a particularly good fantasy, right down to the teasing way she said "punish." Unfortunately, I was sure she didn't mean a teasing, arousing play-punishment followed up by some hot sex. Supervillains didn't play with safewords.

Which didn't keep my pussy from clenching. Fear and arousal were a heady, potent combination.

"What's your master plan, Samhain Kiss?" I demanded, forcing myself to sound stern and confident when inside I was a mess of fear and desire.

"Oh, no, darling, I'll never tell," she purred. "I'm not like those old-time villains who couldn't stop themselves from prancing around and revealing everything before they slipped up and were defeated."

Damn. She had to be all modern and intelligent. Of course, that's also what made her a worthy opponent.

"Of all my enemies, you've been my favorite," she admitted, her dark eyes wide. She licked her lips. A sapphire stud glinted in her nose. "I just *adore* that outfit. I had no idea PVC could be so... malleable. Just look at your sweet little nipple—it looks like it's trying to drill its way through."

Embarrassment and desire thrummed through me, because I knew she was right. I had no opportunity to look, though, because she fastened her mouth on my breast. The material muffled her caressing lips and flicking tongue, transmitting their heat but not the full sensations.

When she bit down, though... *damn* I felt that, a delicious almost-pain. I stifled a moan and pressed my hips down so they wouldn't arch up, seeking contact with something, anything. I couldn't let her know how much my foolish body wanted to get lost in her, since I was sure that was her plan.

A wicked, devious plan.

She moved on to the other nipple, sucking and teasing through the PVC, then sinking her teeth into the hard, covered peak.

It just wasn't enough. I wanted more...

...and a moment later I questioned that desire, when she pulled back and in a blur of motion brought the crop down on my defenseless, pouting nipple.

My hips jerked off the bed as true pain and full arousal shot through me. The sharp sting in my throbbing nipple quickly faded to a wonderful ache. My clit echoed, throbbing and aching in rhythm.

My mind still knew, barely, that Samhain Kiss was my archenemy, but my body betrayed me.

She did it again to my other breast, and I writhed and pulled at my restraints, keening through clenched teeth. More heat, more ache, more need throbbing between my legs. Lightning-fast, she struck me again and then again. I recited my Superhero Oath over and over to keep me from dropping into a place where my mind would also forget who she was, forget who I was, forget everything but lust.

And then, oh God oh God, she trailed the crop down my belly again, and laid it against my crotch. I sucked in a terrified, pleading breath.

Could my superpowers save me?

Could my superheroine PVC panties protect me?

Did I want them to?

Insane as it sounds, it all came together in my head a moment before the crop landed and I came, too.

Agony, oh sweet Lord yes, but unfocused and spread out, transmuted by PVC and desire into ecstasy. The reverberations on my swollen clit were what sent me screaming into orgasm, what set me on fire, what sparked my magical flames.

My superpower roared through me, searing the leather cuffs at my hands and feet. As the ashes fell, I was reaching out to a stunned Samhain Kiss, pulling her down on the bed and flipping myself over on top of her.

Then I put my mouth on hers and fought Samhain Kiss's kiss with Healing Fire's fire.

She resisted at first, of course, but I brought my hand between her legs and found that under her tattered skirt and silvery fishnets, she wore just a scrap of a thong, which served as no protection or barrier.

A scrap of *soaking* thong. Oh, she'd enjoyed her game with me, yes she had. Delight surged through me. I could work with that.

As tempting as it was to pick up the discarded crop and return the favor, I wanted more, now, faster. I plunged a finger into her wetness, then two, then three, grinding my thumb against her clit and fucking her with my hand as I fought with her mouth and breathed my curative power into her.

She came as only an archvillainess can, howling and screaming and nearly breaking my fingers off, or would have if I hadn't had superstrength. And when she was done, I had the curious sense that she was different.

She brought her hand to her face.

"Huh," she said. "It's back to my original stud, isn't it?"

The sapphire had been replaced by a ruby, which went better with her black hair—hair that now, I noticed, no longer had blue streaks in it.

"You had a Distraction *Nose Stud?*"

"Crazy, isn't it?" She giggled. Samhain Kiss might have a throaty laugh like pure sexy evil, but she didn't giggle in that nervous but still sexy way. "I guess that means I'm back to being me. I'm Stacy O'Malley, by the way."

"Maya Simkin." Because I *was*. Our outfits had magically disappeared. Had I defeated Samhain Kiss? For now, at least, I had. Whether her uniform would transfer to a new person, I didn't know.

What mattered was that we were both back to our normal selves, and naked, and still very, very aroused.

Of course, the loss of our super-outfits meant we had no clothes at all, but that was a problem to be solved later.

Much later.

Full blown, full bloom, the color of blood, the color of lips and lovers in heat. Every petal a tongue, a whisper-kiss, a velvety brush of skin in the gloaming. Dipping his nose into its center, brushing his lips along the edges of the petals, he inhaled. The scent was heady and heated, skin and secret places sweating in the throes of passion. It smelled dirty and ripe.

He should have known it was enchanted. No rose grew like that, perfect and sordid, pristine and soiled, without at least a little magic. Perfectly at its peak, ready to be plucked.

But he felt enchanted too—the night quiet as a forest, the garden he'd stumbled into, the secret opening of the rose, surely it all meant something magical and true—and so he bent and did just as the rose asked, using his hunting knife, severing the stem in a single, confident cut.

"What gives you the right...?" At his shoulder, behind him and in front of him all at once. Never a voice like that in all in his years. Growl and snarl around the word, shivers up his spine. "...to steal my best thing?"

He stood still, so still, as if the voice might not be able to see him, clutching a knife in one hand and a rose in the other.

"Well? Explain yourself."

Exhale, the knife hilt sweaty in his fingers. Rose thorns pricking his other palm.

"It's for my... daughter," he said faintly. Voice all breath and plea.

"You no longer have a daughter."

Never lie to those with magic. He knew this. Of course he did.

"I had a daughter," he said. "Once." It was true.

"But this rose is not for her, is it?" The voice closer, impossible not to feel as a shiver up his spine, as a dry snarl against his ear.

"No," he said.

"You know the penalty, do you not, for stealing?"

The hands came with the voice this time, big and ragged, fingers grasping the edges of his hips.

"My daughter," he said.

"Gone," the voice in his ear, lips and teeth around the curl of

Enchanted
Shanna Germain

it. "I want something else. You're to be mine for as long as I like...."

From behind him the hands tightened, pulling him backward. Through his clothes, he felt the heat and size of the creature, the pulsing length of him, already hard and eager. It made his body respond in kind, a desperate groan of want and lust. To be touched, to be handled and plucked. De-petaled. Deflowered.

Teeth sharp at his neck, a row of thorns pressing into his flesh. He leaned into it, the cut and pain of it. A hand—giant, rough— found his erection, gripped its length through the fabric. The knife tumbled from his grasp, the rose stuck in his palm by its thorns alone.

"Let me..." he said. He wanted to ask, *Let me see you. Let me kiss you. Let me lick the edges of your claws, tongue the fur of your legs, suck the sweat and salt from your skin.* But it was too much to say and he was already groaning things that were not words.

"Come with me," the voice said.

"Yes," he said. His hips slid and rocked with the gripping hand, a rising pleasure that made no words. That made him the rose, petals opening, pushing out into being.

The voice sounded different, the teeth less sharp. "Maur, come with me."

Maur. Maur. Maur. The name on his tongue. Whose?

"I stole your rose, for my daughter," he said. His voice like crying. Not like crying. No. "I stole your——"

"Maurice, come back to me. Please."

He shook his head, tears blurring and sliding away. At the movement, the smell of fear and his own stink rushed his nose, overpowering the dirt and soil of the flower. Behind him, the noise of the city rushed back in, sudden and sordid. The honk and careen of traffic, the wail of a siren, somewhere a child crying. Maurice looked at his feet: cement below them, not a knife but a rusted spoon—where had he picked that up? In his hand, a pale red rose, severed at the tip, its edges bug-eaten and blackened. A single red stream of blood flowing down his arm. The siren, coming closer, blaring.

"Bare? Baret?" His mouth barely making words, only that word, that name he knew. That name that belonged to the man he knew, the man he loved.

"I'm here," the voice in his ear, the arms around him, solid and real. "I'm here."

Baret knew the wolf was hunting him. He'd seen it before, knew its teeth and its jaw, the speed of its passage through the mossed, moonlit forest. The vision in his left eye blurred, made the trees slide by like stock-still beasts. He couldn't feel his feet. The crunch and crack of broken things from behind him, catching pace. Half blind, Baret ducked his head and ran, breath huffing, burning his chest.

Silence and the scrape of teeth against his neck, tightening. A growl of capture and ownership. Baret felt himself fall from the impact, tried to catch himself. And went down on his knees in the mossy dirt, claws raking at his back. He shuddered, closed his eyes. No running, no more running, not now.

The wolf knew him, had always known him. It roared his name in its ancient tongue, its face slanted sideways, its maw the language of a hundred years. Broken, he bent and welcomed it, the sting of its claws on his skin, the clamp of its jaw.

He panted into the soft dirt, kneeling and naked, the clothes ripped from him, the heat of the beast upon his back. Prey. He was prey. He lowered himself, elbows down, let the wolf take from him what it wanted. Roared and howled and gave his throat up to the pleasure and the pain.

"Bad girl," the wolf said. "Dirty, naughty girl."

"Yes," Baret said. He was, somehow, all of those things. Other things, dark things. He wanted the wolf to know them all, to pull his secrets from him like pulling treats from a basket, flowers from the fields.

"I'm going to have to eat you." The wolf's breath sweated his skin.

"Yes," Baret said. He knew it was true. He'd eaten something himself, hadn't he? Something that had brought the wolf to his door, set the creature on his path. This was his punishment. His reward.

The teeth, the tongue, his skin suckled deep into that hot maw. Swallowed whole. He was becoming nothing, nothing but blood and marrow.

He buried his hands in the hair of the wolf, the soft curls, the blue eyes. The soil became rug, the wolf howls became animalistic groans of his name.

"Eat you," said the wolf who was Maurice, its mouth already gobbling him down.

"Mirror, mirror, on the wall..." There was more to the rhyme, but Maurice couldn't remember how it went or what the fragment belonged to. The mirror was cracked, or maybe that was his face. The split through his eye, the way one side of his mouth turned down. Split by a line of snow. He leaned into the cold and inhaled it. Freeze. Ice. Cold as stars, twinkling.

"Mirror, mirror," he began again, and this time the mirror answered.

"You are the fairest of them all."

A woman with an apple, a man he knew once upon a time. The apple, shined and perfect, glamored, surely.

"For me?" Maurice asked, thought he asked. He wanted it more than he'd ever wanted anything. He tried to say he would trade his shiny mirror, his split-up face—his fingers in his hair over and over, like a treacherous comb.

But the apple was coming toward him already, in the woman's hand. Maurice opened his mouth wide, wider, bit deep. His mouth was full of round and red, his head tight with it.

"Now," the woman said. "Stop asking the damn mirror. Look at me."

Maurice looked. The woman stood in her red dress, a corset tight around her waist. Transparent shoes made of what looked like glass on her feet. The rustle of the fabric, the touch of that heel to his skin more than he could bear. He tried to say so, but his mouth was full, so full, jaw stretched to groaning. The apple pressed on his tongue, held in place by magic, her magic.

The woman took his mirror, took it for her own. Lipstick around and around a red mouth, smacking lips. He wanted those lips, that red like candy, like apples, like rubies.

The lips disappeared, went away. Reappeared on his body. Everywhere at once. Bite and suckle and drag. Maurice tried to say the pleasure, sometimes the pain, but nothing would come out, nothing but spittle and rasped breath around the apple, nothing but the throat-grunts of his body as he arced into the heat of that red, red mouth.

"You," the woman said after, wiping her mouth, lipstick smearing her hand, her arm, taking the apple from him, letting him breathe again, "are the fairest thing I've ever fucking seen."

Undressing, not a woman anymore without the red dress, the glass shoes, the star-filled voice. Maurice kneeling on the mirror, his mouth open around something else, hot and pulsing, streaming into him, cutting off his very breath.

"Baby, you're so beautiful. I don't know how long I can wait." Baret said it but knew he didn't mean it. He would wait forever, if he had to. Longer. But sometimes he had to say it, even if he was only saying it in the dark of night to the motionless form beside him. "How long do I have to wait?"

Only breathing answered him, the slow, stuttered push of air.

His princess, perfect, still, white skin on white sheets. It had been a hundred years, surely. A million, since she'd been awake. He was her prince; he would wait. He would wait. He would wait.

He'd rubied her lips, seven layers of red. Laid her out in her best dress, blue to match her eyes. With long sleeves, so you couldn't see the pinpricks. Her favorite necklace, woven black leather, a silver clasp.

The needle beside her, empty now. Prick of the spindle. They'd been warned. And still, the point had found them, had stuck them both.

Panic in his chest that she wouldn't wake this time. That a hundred years had come and gone and he'd missed them.

"Wake up," he said. "Wake up."

He'd forgotten how to wake her.

A kiss, she needed. A breath.

He leaned to kiss that perfect face, the breathless lips. Exhaled into her, to warm her. That ice-queen face, that colorless complexion.

Beneath him, movement, a kiss returned. Drowsy at first, growing insistent, groaning. His beautiful princess arching up into him. Baret's heart a million miles an hour in his chest, a galloping horse through briars.

"Oh," his princess said, opening her eyes, blue gaze on him. "My handsome prince. You came."

"I've been waiting and waiting." He sounded petulant, didn't mean to. This is what princes did. Waited long and longer.

"You saved me," she said. Her hand groped, found the needle. He pushed it away with his knee.

"No," he said.

"Once more," she said. "Just one more."

He couldn't deny her anything.

"One for you," she said. "One for me."

The spindle's glitter, silver and cold.

"Just a pinprick," he said.

Lifting her knees, pulling the dress up. Baret's hands already doing the work they knew. No matter how long he waited, he would always know this. He lifted her legs, her ass, found the place that was just for him, the tiny puckered scar.

"Just a little prick," Baret said again and again, pushing deep. "Just a little pinprick."

In two tiny rings, there is so much gold. Sometimes the shine of it makes their eyes hurt, their heads gleam on the inside, that place where the drugs have lived. No one talks about drug rehab in fairy tales. In Once Upon a Time, there are no drugs. There is only magic. Princes. True love. Happily ever after.

"I want it back," Maurice says.

"Me too," Baret says.

Neither of them mean it, but it's something they say as if to ward it off, to keep that book closed and on the shelf.

They've been clean eight months. This world is startling in its thereness. They are startling to themselves in their thereness.

They hold each other, marvel at the real weight of bodies, the heft of time and history that they tried to forget. Maurice's dead daughter, the car accident that has left his face split and scarred. Baret's bad eye, from his father's long-ago hands, the way his stutter comes back sometimes, shakes him into silent tears.

Maur lets his head rest upon Baret's shoulder, the muscle beneath it, the heat of his skin. He plays his fingers along the tangled hair on Baret's chest, thinking: beauty with teeth, thorned thicket, briar patches, poisoned apples. He licks the stubble on Baret's chin, notices the strands where it's turned white, like swans, like snow. He shakes the thought away, buries himself in biting the curve of Baret's neck.

Baret fingers Maur's half-hard cock, remembers, knowing that memory is overpainted with the gold leaf of desire, the time they fucked in the bed with a hundred mattresses, the time they fucked in bear suits, and that orgy with seven other guys. He remembers them all and doesn't care. Here is Maurice, growing hard beneath his touch. Here is Maurice, leaning in to kiss him, tonguing his tongue, growling against his mouth. Wolf, Baret thinks. Wicked queen. And he, too, shakes it away.

"Say my name," Maur says, insistent against his mouth. "Say it. Say it."

And Baret says it three times, slow so there's not a stutter, biting the skin of Maurice's lip between each.

"N-now mine," Baret says.

And Maur does, three times fast, as if he is afraid he might forget.

They move into each other, cock and fist and mouth and skin. The circle of one body to another, spinning not gold but a simpler kind of treasure.

This, they've learned, is how to say I love you. How to keep from tearing yourself in two. How to break the curses of bad apples and poisoned needles and a history that repeats forever.

This, here, now, with the birds talking outside, the gold shine of their rings, the roses in square drinking glasses on the bedside table, the windows like mirrors to another world, moving against each other as if they are two stories trying to be told at this same time—this is neither once upon a time nor happily ever after.

This, here, now, is the truest, hardest, sweetest story of all.

A slit of a window, a bar on the door. A room three paces long, two paces wide. No furniture besides a bed and small dresser, both built by her father. A chamber pot, thank the Lord. Mercy knows these things well, but it is her ritual to check and check them again whenever he locks her in like this.

She opens the curtains and presses her eye to the window. Through the slats attached across the outside, she can just see the path beside the house, and beyond it, the cairn atop the haunted hill. Its white stones gleam in the evening light. The groans from there carry on the wind, reaching Mercy even in her prison of a home. Her spine tingles and her insides itch. She sighs and leans her forehead against the tiny opening to the outside world. A tuft of fresh air blesses her skin.

She waits as long as she can, then paces. Three steps for the length, two for the width. Three steps for the length, two for the width. Her best hope is to wear herself out. Sleep consumes unbearable hours.

For now, she prays. *Sweet Jesus, dear Savior, why did God create me beautiful as the devil? Why would He place me on His green earth for no purpose other than tempting men from His commandments?* Mercy has barely seen herself, but these are her father's words. He shouts them whenever his fingers close around her upper arm to drag her to this room and shut her in.

She still wears her hat, her going-out clothes. He let her accompany him to the general store today. She should have known better than to accept the offer. People had looked at her there. Her father had seen them lusting after her.

Mercy has often wondered why her father has not given her in marriage, making her someone else's problem. She is long past the age. But seven years ago, her father sent Jeremiah Chittwood away empty-handed, followed by Thomas Parker soon after. Three years ago, he beat Adam Thetcher to a bloody pulp. No one has come to ask for her since.

The sun has yet to dip past the horizon, but Mercy already wants a drink of water. It's useless to pound on the door and beg,

The Mistress Under the Hill
Annabeth Leong

but she tries it anyway. She wonders how long before he lets her out. The worst was three days, and she'd been sick for a week after.

She gives up hope and sits on the edge of the bed. Mercy often wonders what it would be like to have a husband. She closes her eyes and passes the time with a familiar game.

"I love you," she whispers.

"And I you." Her own voice, lowered and disguised. Mercy reaches out to the side and clutches the bedspread, imagining fingers, smooth and strong and interlaced with hers. She concentrates as hard as she can on the sensation of skin. It would be warm. She would feel a few hairs from the man's fingers. He might stroke the back of her hand with a callused thumb.

"Shall we go to bed?"

"By all means. I long for you."

Mercy eases the hat off her head, tendrils of her red hair falling down beside her chin. "Why don't you undress me?" She likes the sound of her voice in that sentence, both sweet and coy. She tries it out a few times, a few different ways, tasting the breath of it. "Why don't you undress me? Why don't you undress me?"

Her hands tremble on their way to the top button of her high-necked wool gown. She strokes first beneath her jaw. Her husband would begin by tilting her face up to his. Mercy presses lips to palm, the barest touch. For all her husband's gentleness, she would feel his barely restrained desire for her.

Her hands snap back to her collar, tugging it so the rough fabric scrapes the soft skin of her throat. Mercy undoes the first button, then the second, smoothing the mulberry material out of the way after each. Her fingertips flutter down the side of her neck, teasing. Her heart pounds hard. She pauses, allowing her pulse to surge rhythmically against her fingers.

"Please," Mercy breathes. "Don't stop there."

She struggles to reach the buttons running down the back of her dress. She flops onto the bed, rolling and tangling her skirts between her legs. She would writhe against her husband while he freed her from these clothes. She can't imagine holding still beneath his touch.

Slowly, methodically, one button and one string at a time, Mercy releases her breasts, the pressure of her clothes around her rib cage gradually letting up and then disappearing. The cloth rustles as it slips away, and Mercy maneuvers herself onto her back, her upper half naked and chilly in the lonely room.

Eyes still squeezed shut, she touches her bare skin, prodding delicately at the soft swells of flesh rising from her chest. She weighs her breasts in her hands, guiding them up and down, left and right. She circles her palms lightly over her nipples, the satin skin on the tip of each breast growing rougher as it tightens and hardens to little pointed nubs.

Mercy wishes she could give a face to this husband. She wants to see his concentration as he transforms her this way, his admiration for her beauty, the love in his eyes. But it's not the clerk at the general store she wants, or Thomas Parker. Jeremiah Chittwood has grown thick at the jowls and round of belly since the days he sought her hand, and she can no longer summon the image of Adam Thetcher without also seeing his swollen eyelids and broken nose. She shakes her head to banish the disturbing memory and lets the man of her daydream remain vague.

"Pinch me," Mercy says, and clamps down on her left nipple, twisting and tugging. The sensation of her own firm grip radiates through her body, tightening her throat and lungs and causing her hips to lift into the air. She crushes it harder between her thumb and the side of her first finger, biting her lip to keep the voice out of her gasps. Mercy tries the other one, drifting her eyes open now to watch the dark pink flesh stretch away from her breast and then snap back into place.

She slaps one palm against each breast sharply enough to sting her taut nipples, and waits a beat to make sure she hasn't caught her father's attention. Hearing no sound from the rest of the house, she proceeds to squeeze with all her strength, gritting her teeth to hold in the moan forming in the back of her throat. "I love you," she sighs.

Quickly now, Mercy struggles out of the rest of her clothing, kicking the hump of it away and off the bed. She rests a little, enjoying the ache in her breasts as she tickles the sides of her stomach with her fingers.

Then it is time for her secret discovery. Mercy tries to draw the moment out, feathering touches over her inner thighs and scraping her fingernails across her hips, but she can only hold back so much. Setting her jaw firmly, she imagines her arms around her dream husband. He holds her just as tightly. In her mind, Mercy wraps herself around him in every way she can, as firmly as she can.

Her right hand forms a fist and she slides it to the place between her legs. She nestles her fist against the heat and stickiness there and presses hard. Her hips find the rhythm on their own, sliding and working against Mercy's hard, round fist, rubbing those soft, humid parts against it. The sensations begin between her legs, but soon spread, extending into her lower belly and down her inner thighs. Mercy's body goes rigid. She points her toes. She grunts softly in the back of her throat.

Her fantasy forgotten, the winding, straining pleasure of the movement drives her on, teaching her what to do and how to move. Finally, Mercy gives a long, loud exhale as the pleasure lifts to a breaking point and pulses through her body. She rolls onto her side with her legs pressed together as tight as a vise around her fist, drinking the feeling down to the dregs.

Mercy pants. A drop of sweat rolls across her hairline. The smell of her body fills the room, and now she hopes her father will take his time releasing her, waiting long enough for some of this pungent odor to dissipate. But it's not an unpleasant scent to her. She relaxes her fist and brings the side of her hand up to her nose, breathing herself in.

She wants water desperately, but the strong smell centers and calms her. It's a way of lingering inside the bursting moment of pleasure, when she has no worries and knows the grace of God. She is safe within her secret discovery, beyond the reach of her father and his strange, strict rules.

Mercy treasures the sensation as her eyes focus and she comes back to herself, sitting up carefully in the bed.

"Lovely," says a voice—a real voice—and Mercy is too frightened even to scream. She snatches her dress from the floor and holds it crumpled against her breasts.

"Well, don't do that," the voice murmurs. It comes from the tiny slits in the window. "Beauty such as yours should remain unbound."

"Who are you?" Mercy manages to stammer.

"Come and see."

She crosses the tiny room, lifting one eye to the largest space between the slats. She and the bearer of the voice would be pressing their faces together if not for the wall between them.

He is flesh and blood, with none of the usual color to sweeten the deal. White flesh, red irises, hair the shade of cobwebs. Short for a man, he strains up onto his toes to reach the window.

But she feels his breath, warm against her upper lip and smelling of the damp world outside the house.

"You needn't fear me," the man tells Mercy. "I have observed without permission, but my transgressions go no further. I require your invitation for all else."

"It's for you I fear," Mercy says. She explains about Adam Thetcher.

"You need fear for me even less than for yourself." He laughs. The sound barely remains on the sane side of madness, the sort of noise that makes one wish the evening light would not leave so soon.

"I owe you a favor, Mercy Broome," he says, and she does not need to ask how he knows her name. "I must make a fair trade for what I took from you."

She smiles doubtfully. "What favor can you give, considering all that separates us?"

"Have you seen a man, Mercy?" When she does not respond, he continues. "Wouldn't you like to?"

His fingers crawl to the buttons of his shirt. Mercy holds her breath. She should stop him, but the pounding still between her legs says she cannot. True, he is not beautiful as Jeremiah Chittwood once was, but where are her pretty suitors now? This man unveils himself before her.

The man uncovers a small, powerful body. Pale, curling hairs start at the base of his neck and thatch his chest. In the dying day, harsh shadows form below his rounded pectoral muscles, almost obscuring his equally chiseled stomach and the stirring dimly visible within his trousers.

The stranger discards his clothes on the ground outside Mercy's window without a care, never taking his piercing, predatory eyes from her face. He runs the flats of his hands down his sides, defining his shape for her. Below his stout chest, his waist seems narrow as a girl's, but his thighs sprout thick as young trees.

Her eyes follow the movements of his fingertips. He smiles knowingly and toys with her gaze. Now coy, he displays the layers of scars at the points of his elbows. Now lewd, he cups the heavy sack that hangs between his legs, lifting and stroking it for her. Hanging before it is his hardening cock. She notes the blunt head, its slitted eye, the thick pink stalk. With dramatic gestures, the man draws it out, lengthening it and bringing it to life before Mercy's eyes.

Her fingers shake, wound in the lattice of slats over the window in an unconscious effort to get closer, to touch as well as look.

He grins as if reading her mind and spits on the palm of his hand. Rubbing and polishing the knob at the end of his pole of flesh, the stranger breaks gaze with Mercy for the first time, his eyelids falling closed. A wrinkle forms on the bridge of his nose, and she recognizes his need to concentrate on pleasure, budding and burgeoning.

The man's free hand extends, the fingers curled into a strange, spasmodic position. The other wraps fully around his cock, the tease fading from his movements, replaced by focus.

Mercy's curious eyes devour him. His head sinks low in his pleasure, taut shoulders hunched up around his ears, the muscles cording in his neck. He rocks his hips into his hand, rises onto his toes, breathes heavily through his nose. The tip of his tongue, alarmingly red, just breaks the seal of his lips at the left corner, twitching slightly as he jerks himself.

Then his mouth pops open with one ragged moan. Thick white cords of fluid spurt from the tip of his cock, arcing from his body in a series of pulses.

Slowly, he opens his eyes, holding up one messy hand for her inspection. Mercy squirms on her side of the wall, locked away by the window and her father's control. She pokes her nose out through the opening and he understands, bringing his hand close enough for her to smell. The salt of air blown west from the sea floods Mercy's senses. For a moment, she can remember the sun breaking from the constant gray above.

Mercy hesitates, then flicks out her tongue, just grazing the tip against the sticky fluid on his hand. Withdrawing to her mouth, she savors the speck of flavor, thick and bitter. Not a child's flavor. Mercy tastes the woman's life she has been denied.

"Lovely," the stranger says again. He remains naked. Mercy slowly lets fall the clump of clothes she's been holding against herself. Longing bursts through her, centered in the depths of her stomach, but radiating far beyond.

The stranger's gaze feels like fingers, stroking her everywhere. Mercy sighs aloud.

"Come with me," the man says. "Be my bride, the mistress under the hill. I will do anything you ask."

His gaze shifts. He squints. Mercy glances over her shoulder, following his eyes. She can't see through walls, but she knows in her gut that he's staring directly at her father. She shivers. The stranger steps closer to the window. All she sees now are his red, blood-filled lips. "Anything you ask," he repeats.

She wants. She dreams. She cannot.

Mercy leaps forward and draws the curtains closed. She sits on the bed, hands wrapping her chest, gasping until she's sure the stranger has moved on.

A brow twisted as wind-battered trees looms above Mercy. Her father's fierce blue left eye glares down at her, measuring and disapproving. The other eye, made of glass, simply stares. He slaps her cheek, the sting light. He's not really angry at her.

"Dress yourself properly, girl."

Mercy clears her dry throat, stretches her cracked lips. She crawled into her clothes after the stranger left, but her skirts are tangled now from hours of tossing in her bed, feverish and thirsty. She pulls herself back from her father, wrapping herself in a ball in the shadow of the bed's headboard. She nods.

"You look like a horror," he says.

"I'm sorry." Her voice sounds unfamiliar.

"Goody Keyne will come to dinner tonight. You've a lot to do to get the house ready."

Mercy can't speak any more. She stands to show her readiness, all too aware of every wrinkle in her dress and the stench of her unwashed body. She lurches, dizzy from her head's rapid change in elevation. Her father studies her, sneers, and leaves the room.

Goody Keyne talks endlessly of the gospels, but she never gives her opinion on anything in them. Mercy sits patiently through her rendition of the Sermon on the Mount, and then a description of the thoughts of many preachers on the subject. Mercy's father praises the old woman for her memory, her fine choice of words, and her devotion.

Mercy sips her drink as slowly as she can manage, not wanting to call attention to the raging thirst she still feels. She knows from experience that it will take a few days for it to pass, unless she wishes to risk being accused of gluttony in order to slake it.

When her father at last sees Goody Keyne to the door, Mercy allows herself to deflate. She retreats to her room and shuts the door, only then noticing the fine gown spread over her bed.

It shimmers against the dull brown of her bedclothes. Blue as the late evening sky! Mercy has never seen such a color. It must surely be vanity, and yet she cannot stop herself from touching the fabric, the weave more perfect than anything she could achieve, the thread spun more delicately.

Mercy lifts the dress and hugs it against her chest. Goosebumps rise everywhere the soft fabric touches. Unknown perfume wafts from the material, the expensive scent of a flower too exotic for Mercy to recognize.

Her heart pounding, she undoes her own plain, high-necked dress and replaces it with this new elegant garment. She smooths it over her body. The gown transforms her touch. She gives a powerful shiver. She need not ask herself from whence it came— only one source could explain such a gift.

Mercy experiments, spinning in a circle on the small patch of bare floor in her bedroom. Unsatisfied desire crystallizes in her chest, presenting an image of one compelling transgression.

She does not dare, and yet cannot resist. Before she has time to question herself, Mercy unfastens her bedroom door. She treads lightly as a ghost, and yet the wooden floor still creaks beneath her step. Cringing with every movement, Mercy creeps through the house, where she eases the front door open and steals out.

None of her shoes can reach the level of the gown she wears, and so Mercy walks barefoot. The haunted hill pulls at her bones. She could travel there without looking or thinking.

The night sings with mysteries that Mercy has always been

denied. Gentle buzzes, flashes of unexplained light, and whispering leaves signal that Mercy's secrets will easily blend with the many others that together weave the thick blanket of darkness.

Moist ground kisses the soles of her feet with each step she takes. The smell of earth enfolds her. Moonlight caresses her. Mercy knows he is waiting for her at the hill. Her pace speeds at the thought of him, his pale eyelids blinking over blood-colored eyes. His eyes like wounds, open to the sight of her.

She nears the hill. Pebbles bruise the bottoms of her feet, forcing her into an awkward dance along the path. And music bursts into the night, plunging Mercy into a dance indeed. Apparitions around her twist their bodies into graceful, broken forms, glimpsed from the corner of an eye, perceived by the hairs on the back of the neck.

Mercy rises onto her toes and moves faster still, the beat of the music accelerating with her. Her head spins with the confusion of the movement flashing around her. Her mind can't grasp her surroundings. She glances back toward the house but can't see it through the viscous dark.

Then a hand in hers. "If I may?"

She smiles at him. Their fingers interlace. He guides her into the dance completely, the subtle pressure of his fingers somehow teaching Mercy's feet where to fall. The shapes around her change and clarify. Women in jewel-encrusted gowns. Men in shoes that shine like the moon. But all remain strange—too tall, too thin, too pale, or too dark.

Mercy knows she doesn't belong among these creatures, but then her stranger slides one hand down to the curve of her waist and she relinquishes her fears to the strength of his grip.

"Do you have a name?" Mercy breathes.

"Samuel."

They dance for hours, until Mercy's feet bleed and her knees quiver. Still, she does not want to stop. Samuel senses her weakness, supporting her weight and drawing her closer to him.

"The night will be over soon," he whispers. Mercy shakes her head in disbelief. They dance alone. She did not notice the other creatures retreating, did not see the moon fading before the coming dawn.

"Will you keep the dress and be my bride?" His lips smile against her ear. "Or will you return the gift to me now?"

Mercy freezes in his arms. "Now?"

"Oh, yes. Something of yours must remain at my hill in exchange for what I sacrificed." He grips her hips tightly. "Let it be you. My mistress under the hill. And ask what you will." Again, that significant glance, into the distance this time. Mercy holds no doubt—he stares directly at her father.

Mercy pulls back, and is a little surprised when Samuel lets her go. She hesitates, lifting her fingers to the buttons of the dress but not following through.

"Look at what I did for you," he says. He loosens his own clothes. The marks of teeth purple at his throat. Angry, scabbed scratches mar the sides of his arms, his chest, and his back. The wounds seem to writhe against the canvas of his colorless skin.

"I don't understand."

He steps free of his trousers, his cock a tall, hard cylinder standing out from his body. "Take off the dress."

Mercy shivers and obeys. She peels the sweat-stained dress away from her skin, its expensive scent mingled now with the smell of her own body.

"Look at it," Samuel says.

Mercy glances down, at the wrong side of the fabric. Stains she hadn't noticed bloom across its surface, sticky and fresh. "What did—?"

"Its owner did not give it over easily."

The implications of the rusty color marring the inside of the dress sink in. Mercy screams and thrusts the garment out at arm's length, paying no mind to the chill pre-dawn air playing over her naked body.

Samuel steps closer. She recognizes the smell of his cock. The red of his eyes deepens, mirroring the stains on the dress. "I want to give you what you wish for most of all," he whispers. "Anything you ask. I want to serve you. Please. I need to."

Mercy vibrates with longing. She cannot release her grip on the beautiful dress. Neither can she step back from him.

He lifts a hand toward her face. She waits, but he refrains from contact.

"I can only touch with your permission," he reminds her.

Mercy draws in a shaky breath. Before she can change her mind, she jerks forward, pressing her cheek into his palm. He groans.

"I won't stay," she says quickly. "And I won't keep the dress. But..." She trails one finger over the half-open cuts on his throat. He sucks in a lungful of air. Mercy leans nearer. The tiny hairs on his neck move in response to the rhythm of her exhalations. "I thank you. For everything. For... giving me something fine, wherever it came from. For making me feel pretty." Squeezing her eyes shut, she kisses the wound, rubbing her soft lips across its scabby, ragged edges.

When she pulls back, he's gritting his teeth, both hands fisted at his sides. "What's wrong?"

"Do you think it's easy to follow the rules that separate us?"

Mercy smiles. All her life, her father has warned her about men and their uncontrollable passions, and this is the first time she has been free enough to gather any clue of what he means.

She knows she cannot accept Samuel's offer, even if he is the only man who stands a chance of getting her away from her father. Lord knows what manner of creature he is. Still, she wants him. She notices the dress, clutched forgotten in her extended fist. She lifts it to her face, allowing it to unfurl. It snaps softly in the wind that rushes over the hill.

Mercy takes one of Samuel's hands, forcing the fingers open. His restraint thrills her, a triumph over the lust that vibrates between their naked bodies. Mercy wraps his hand with the stained dress, then releases him.

"Touch me," she whispers, "but only through the dress."

He hisses. She trembles so hard her teeth chatter. Mercy locks her fingers together behind her back to keep from inadvertently resisting.

The soft fabric kisses her throat, but she knows the light touch is only a prelude. Next, he engulfs her right breast in a harsh grip, tugging her so close his breath heats her face and his lips hover just over her cheek. She wonders if he will break her restriction with a kiss, but he does not. He holds her on the razor's edge of it, squeezing her breast ever tighter.

Mercy's head spins. She barely remembers to breathe. He shifts to her nipple, the dress seeming rough now compared to that soft skin. It hurts, but it also makes her ache.

She meets his eyes and grabs his wrist, guides his hand down between her legs. The wad of the garment presses against her most sensitive place, backed by his firm hold. Mercy braces her hands on his shoulders and grinds her hips to please herself.

Samuel holds steady, maintaining even pressure for her to buck against. Mercy's juices wet the fabric, softening the sensation as she rubs against it. She adds another stain to it, willingly.

It is hard to keep her eyes on Samuel. She wants to slip into her private world of fantasy, the place where she has always been safe. But she resists. She wants to bring him into her, and so she keeps her eyes open to him, imagining that he can see through them to the images that run through her head.

She pictures his mouth covering one breast and then the other, biting and kissing, confusing pain and pleasure. She would spread herself for him but tremble, wanting and fearing him, never certain if his next touch will bring kindness or cruelty.

Standing before her, Samuel smiles slightly. As if he knows. She shivers at the idea of him entering her mind. It's so close to the other forbidden thought she has—of his cock thrusting into her body. Mercy presses the side of her face against his, breathing in the damp earth aroma that rises from his chilly, pale skin. She sighs and comes, shuddering against his cloth-covered hand.

His limbs stay in place, but air charges in and out of his lungs. Against her cheek, his jaw shifts. He grinds his teeth, a soft growl rising in the back of his throat. "If you will leave me tonight, let it be now," he says.

Still feeling the clenching glow of her release, Mercy pulls back. Water in the eyes belies Samuel's fierce expression. She feels a rush of affection that frightens her more than the idea of what he did to get the dress.

The early call of a bird reminds her that dawn will break any moment, and she is naked. Mercy nods once to Samuel and flees toward her house as if the devil himself pursues her. She wonders if he does.

The house seems to sleep. Mercy creeps closer with increasing trepidation. She knows how she looks.

Light and barefoot as she is, she makes noise every step. Twigs crack, or Mercy hisses in pain as a stone presses up into the wounds on her soles. It's more light than dark by now, and every second brings more of the sun's blaze.

She steals to the front door, wincing at the creaking of the half-rotten outside stairs. She can guide it open silently, she tells herself, and race to her room and climb into her bed before her father is the wiser.

Holding her breath, she tries it, as slowly and carefully as a stalking woodsman. She takes her time. Not a sound escapes from the big, wooden door. Mercy smiles to herself and enters the house.

"Whore!"

She flinches and shrinks back, but her father yanks her inside and slams the door. His seeing eye squints but the skin around his glass eye can't mirror the expression. He glares lopsided and monstrous at Mercy's bleeding feet and exposed body.

"All these years," he whispers. "I feared for you. I protected you. And how do you treat me now?"

Mercy lifts her chin. She has never talked back to him, but

words burn inside her throat. "You hurt people who had committed no sin against me or you." Adam Thetcher. Had she loved him? It is impossible to say now—the thought of him brings so much guilt.

"Were you the sinner, then? I knew it from your youth. I gave life to a Delilah." He touches her hair for a moment, but snatches his hand back as if seared. "Red hair and green eyes. The devil's blood must have come from your mother's line." He covers his face with both hands. "And a shape that would destroy a man!" He stumbles away from the door. "Go to your room!" he screams.

Mercy hangs her head, intending to obey, but cannot bring herself to move. It's not been a full day since her last stint locked up and starving. She hasn't the strength or the will.

"Go! Now!"

"No," Mercy whispers.

"What?"

"No." Her voice strengthens. "You will not confine me again. I have done no wrong."

For a moment, she questions herself. Has not her behavior with Samuel been thoroughly wicked? And yet the thought holds no force for Mercy. She has long wished for matrimony. She dreamt for years of sharing herself with a husband. But her father has punished her with one hand for not taking the path he denies her with the other. No. Mercy will please herself from now on, without apology.

She stands tall and faces her father. He stares as if he doesn't know her. She can't look away from his glass eye, so wide and unfeeling, holding no sympathy for her at all.

She knows what he will do a moment before the first blow strikes, and braces herself as best she can. Not good enough. Mercy falls to the floor. She curls into a ball. The beating continues with heavy, dull strikes along her spine. Mercy tries to crawl away. No escape.

She throbs into consciousness. The bed she lies in hurts. The light of the sun hurts. Breathing hurts. Being awake inside her body hurts. She opens her eyes, wailing at the familiar sight. A faint glow through the slit of a window. A bar on the door. The dull, familiar ceiling. The bed, the dresser, and the spot of floor.

She is thirsty already. Mercy sits up, gasps at the pain in her head, and drops back down.

"I have a gift for you," a familiar voice says, from inside the room this time. Mercy gives a little scream and gets up despite her body's protests. Her father must have dressed her before putting her to bed, and the stiff, plentiful fabric that covers and chokes her bruised skin creates pain in its own right.

"Samuel?" He is shadowed in the corner, sitting like a little boy with his knees drawn up under his chin. He regards her with eyes that appear all the more bloody considering his haggard face.

"It is the best gift I could find." He opens a hand, holding it out to Mercy. On his palm sits a finger, adorned with a fine ruby ring. Mercy knows that she should ask where this has come from, but he looks so distressed that she forgets even her own pain and kneels on the floor before him, one hand stroking his white hair.

"What happened to you?"

He is shaking. He thrusts his open palm at her more insistently. "Take the gift and make the trade. Come with me to be mistress under the hill." He shuts his eyes, the accusation in his voice aimed in all directions. "You should not have left when last we met. You should not have."

Mercy peers at the finger in his hand. Diamonds swirl around the ruby. Someone lovingly carved an inscription in the gold of the ring: "Autre ne veut." She frowns at the foreign words. She wrinkles her nose at the smell of the lady's finger. Mercy does not want to think about this.

Gently, she lifts the finger from his hand and sets it beside him on the floor. "How did you get inside?"

"I had to be near you. Even if I could not help you." He glares at his hands, clenching and unclenching them.

"Why?"

"How many times must I ask you to be my bride? Do you not understand my feelings? I will do anything you ask, and yet you do not ask." This time, he does not look beyond her. He keeps his eyes on her, and his meaning remains crystal clear.

Mercy shudders. He transforms the aching of her body from pain to longing. She leans forward slowly, her bruises twinging despite her care. She guides her lips to his and waits there. Neither one moves for a while. They hold their pose, breathing each other's breath.

Then her mouth parts, but he will take nothing without explicit permission, and so Mercy presses her tongue through his lips instead. He tastes of blood and dirt and secrets. She moans and kisses harder, beginning to crawl into his lap until she leans her weight on a fearsome bruise and breaks off with a yelp.

She crumples beside him, panting, with tears in her eyes. "I need you to touch me," she whispers. "Please."

She sets no conditions. In the depths of her despair, she cares nothing for her virtue. She has heard that a woman suffers in her first congress with a man, but what pain could Samuel cause her that she does not already feel? She abandons herself to his arms, preparing for his invasion.

He does not ravish her. He lifts her off the floor and carries her to the bed, but when they get there he only strokes her hair.

"I love you," she whispers. It does not matter if it is true.

"And I you." His thumb rubs circles on the back of her hand, softer than her own skin, and cold.

"Why don't you undress me?"

Silence thickens the room, and then his hands tremble their way to the top button of her high-necked wool gown. He stops before unfastening it. One palm runs down the side of her face, just grazing her. She turns to kiss his palm. For all his gentleness, his barely restrained desire burns there beneath her lips, and his anger.

"Please," Mercy breathes. "Don't stop there."

His hands snap back to her collar, tugging it so the rough

fabric scrapes the soft skin of her throat. The first button gives way to his pull, then the second. His fingertips flutter down the side of her neck, and he pricks her with hints of his sharp nails. Her heart pounds hard. He freezes. Her pulse surges rhythmically against his fingers.

Mercy can't hold still beneath his touch. She writhes against Samuel, tangling herself further in the dress, despite her need to be released. Cold, unnaturally smooth lips light against her throat. "Be still," he says.

She obeys, closing her eyes as he peels the dress from her. She sighs as her breasts and ribs come free, and then her stomach. Relieved of the garment's constriction, the thudding pain of her bruises eases.

Cloth whispers above her, and then the wiry hair on his chest rubs against the tender skin of hers. He flings an arm over her, their bodies slightly tacky where they make contact. Mercy smiles and reaches for him, but he is not where she expects.

His lips journey down her body, walking the length of the hard bone between her breasts. He continues, letting her stomach pillow his kisses. He nudges her thighs apart.

The first tap of his tongue against the secret center of her pleasure jerks Mercy nearly upright. Samuel murmurs soothingly, then puts tongue to her again, slower this time. His tongue travels firm and luxurious through the cleft between her legs, coaxing folds of skin apart with barely any pressure at all. Its touch flickers. It could almost be one of Mercy's fantasies, except that she has never imagined such a thing before.

Carefully, as if she might bolt, Samuel's hands wrap around her thighs, holding her in place. He increases the force of his tongue, licking faster now. Three upward strokes, two across, and back again. The regularity of the pleasure lulls and relaxes Mercy. His tongue paces her body the way she used to pace this little bedroom. Its rhythm tells her she has plenty of time.

She gazes at the ceiling and allows him to conduct her at his own pace toward the point of release. Can she truly share this refuge with another? Mercy aches up toward his tongue. Her legs strain but she does not rock the way she wants to.

Samuel's right hand creeps higher up her thigh. He swipes a finger through the liquid pooling between her legs. He runs the tip of his finger around Mercy's opening and presses his tongue flat against her.

Pleasure bursts like a bubble. She grips the back of his head and holds him tight against her. Mercy wishes the world could stop then and there, leaving her frozen in that mind-erasing moment.

Samuel remains patiently in place until she releases him. He lifts his head, his chin glistening with her juices. Mercy leans down and strokes her finger under his lip, gathering up her own wetness. Bringing her hand to her nose, she closes her eyes and breathes her own scent, mingled with the graveyard flavor of Samuel's mouth.

He crawls up her body, his cock hard between them. She meets his strange, red eyes. "What gift will you accept?" Samuel whispers. "In exchange for becoming mistress under the hill?"

Mercy swallows hard. She spreads her legs wide around him. She twists her face to the side, as if she is the one who can see through walls. "One glass eye," she tells him quickly. She turns back in time to see his smile, just before he plunges himself into her waiting body.

Contributors

Shanna Germain claims the titles of writer, editor, game designer, lex-imaven, and Schrodinger's brat. She is the co-owner and creative director at Monte Cook Games, and her work has been widely published in places like *Best American Erotica*, *Best Gay Romance*, *Best Lesbian Erotica*, and *Fantastic Erotica:The Best of Circlet Press* from 2008-2012. Her most recent works include *As Kinky As You Wanna Be*, *The Lure of Dangerous Women*, and *No Thank You, Evil!*

Vivien Jackson: Nerdy girl | Austinite | unrepentant dumpling eater | recovering comma wrangler and which-hunter | writer of salacious kissery | Member RWA, AustinRWA, RWA FF&P, DD, and some other letters | "I aim to misbehave." Always.

Michael M. Jones lives in Southwest Virginia with a pride of cats, too many books, and a wife who warily taste-tests his cookies. He has appeared in numerous Circlet and Cleis anthologies, such as *Fantastic Erotica* and *A Princess Bound*. He is also the editor of *Like a Cunning Plan*, *Like Fortune's Fool*, and *Scheherazade's Facade*, among other collections. He is very sleepy.

Great mystery surrounds the birth of **Beverly Langland**: except that she was born in Llanhilleth, Wales—land of castles and dragons—nothing further is definite. She is not, as most believe, a lesbian living in a man's body. Beverly maintains that a careless probationary nurse mixed the nametags on a group of babies and that she is, in fact, Dr. Walden Roberts, mystery/thriller author. Walden strongly denies this at all times. As they are both married to the same woman, considerable confusion arises. Most of Beverly's published erotic short stories have appeared in print anthologies, though her excursions into the genre are all too rare. Beverly hopes to correct that oversight shortly. Find more about her work at www.beverlyblue.net.

Annabeth Leong wears high heels and frequents the former haunts of H.P. Lovecraft. One month, she is a baseball fanatic, and the next she's reading about squid. She is frequently confused about her sexuality, but enjoys searching for answers. Her work appears in more than 50 anthologies, including *Best Women's Erotica 2015*, *Whispers in Darkness: Lovecraftian Erotica*, *Like a Trip Through the Mirror: Lesbian Love in Alternate Realities*, and *What Lies Beneath: Erotic Horror*. Many of her stories are collected in *Liquid Longing: An Erotic Anthology of the Sacred and Profane*, published by Forbidden Fiction. She is the editor of *MakerSex: Erotic Stories of Geeks, Hackers, and DIY Projects*. Find Annabeth online at annabetherotica.com, and on Twitter @AnnabethLeong

Sophie Mouette: Author of the 4-star (*Romantic Times*) novel *Cat Scratch Fever, Out of the Frying Pan, Possessed, Undressed, and in a Mess*, and many short stories, Sophie Mouette is the brainchild of two widely published authors of erotica, romance, and speculative fiction. The two halves of Sophie—Dayle A. Dermatis (aka Andrea Dale) and Teresa Noelle Roberts—met almost three decades ago at a writers' conference. Talking nonstop, they closed down the hotel bar and went somewhere else to keep on talking. They still are…. For more information, visit her at SophieMouette.com.

Alex Picchetti knows a superhero never reveals their secrets. Previous stories with Circlet include "A World of Her Own" in *Like the Knave of Hearts*, "Midway Rides" in *Like a Vorpal Blade*, and "I Am The Very Model of A Modern Circlet Editor" (with HB Kurtzwilde) in *Like a Circlet Editor*.

Steven Schwartz is a writer of SF/F, a pornographer, a performer, and a book artist. He remembers being obsessed with the D'Aulaire illustrations of the Trojan War myths when he was young, and has always had a taste for eccentric language.

Cecilia Tan is a writer, editor, and sexuality activist. She is the author of *Slow Surrender, The Prince's Boy, Mind Games, The Hot Streak, White Flames, Edge Plays, Black Feathers, The Velderet, and Telepaths Don't Need Safewords*, as well as the Magic University series of paranormal erotic romances. She has the distinction of being perhaps the only writer to have erotic fiction published in both *Penthouse* and *Ms.* magazines, as well as in scores of other magazines and anthologies including

Asimov's, *Best American Erotica*, and *Nerve*. She is the founder and editor of Circlet Press, publishers of erotic science fiction and fantasy, the founder and creator of the Fetish Fair Fleamarket ™, and was inducted into the Saints & Sinners Hall of Fame for GLBT writers in 2010.

Elizabeth Thorne is thrilled to make her living from sex ... writing about it, that is. In addition to her day job creating educational material about sexual health, she has published a wide variety of erotic fiction and non-fiction. Her book of BDSM erotic fairy tales "The Gingerbread Dungeon" is currently available from Lazy Day Publishing, and you can find more of her work at WithBatedBeth.com.

If you enjoyed this book, you might also enjoy...

Superlative Speculative Erotica
edited by Cecilia Tan and Bethany Zaiatz
Twenty of the best erotic science fiction and fantasy stories published by Circlet Presson our 25th anniversary. A little cyberpunk, some high fantasy, a touch of horror, some superheroes, a bit of space opera, some paranormal... What unites these stories is their quality. The anthology also features characters who identify as lesbian, gay, genderqueer, bisexual, trans, and heterosexual. What label do you put on a book like that? We call it... superlative speculative erotica.

Fantastic Erotica
edited by Cecilia Tan & Bethany Zaiatz
To celebrate the 20th Anniversary of Circlet Press, Fantastic Erotica presents the very best erotic science fiction and fantasy short stories published by Circlet in the past five years. Chosen by popular vote by the readership from among all the stories published by Circlet from 2008 to the present, these favorites are the cream of the crop.

Best Fantastic Erotica
edited by Cecilia Tan
The best erotic science fiction and fantasy as determined by the annual contest run by Circlet Press. Rewarding originality and positive sensuality, the contest inspires well-known and unknown writers alike to excel in this provocative genre. Erotic sf/f combines erotic and sexual themes with magic, futurism, high fantasy, cyberpunk, space opera, magic realism, and all the many other sub-genres.

All Genres ⊊+ All Genders

⊊+Circlet Press: Erotica For Geeks www.circlet.com